STRIPPED DOWN

ERIN MCCARTHY

Cover art by Hang Le

Connect with Erin:

Twitter

Facebook

Goodreads

www.erinmccarthy.net

ONE

"I THINK YOU SHOULD ALL STRIP," Lilly Ferguson said with a firm nod.

Rick Ryder raised his eyebrows at his friend. "Lil, you've gotten kinky in your old age." They say if you live long enough you see everything, and hell, here he was at only twenty-eight, witnessing their most uptight female friend asking to see their junk at four in the afternoon.

She rolled her eyes at him. Which was reassuring.

Sullivan O'Toole looked unnerved from his position behind the bar. "What are you talking about, Lilly?"

"Hear me out." Lilly was on a worn stool at Tap That, Sullivan's bar in their hometown of Beaver Bend, Minnesota.

Lil was between Rick and their other decade-long friend, Axl, who was still in uniform, having just gotten off duty at the Beaver Bend Police Department, and who looked more like Rick felt—amused.

"What is there to hear?" Sullivan asked. "Damn, Lil, you just asked us to take off our clothes. Do we need to download a dating app for you?"

She threw a swizzle stick at him. "Not for personal reasons!

Ew. Get your ego in check. I mean for a charity strip event. Like a Magic-Mike-style routine. We can call you the Tap That Dancers. You, Rick, Axl, Jesse, and Brandon. I'll choreograph the routine and we'll make a ton of money for breast cancer research." Lilly smiled, looking pleased with herself as she tucked her dark hair behind her ear.

Stripping for charity. Much more in character than Lilly getting up close and personal with them. Rick gave her a grin, because he thought it could be a fun way to distract Sullivan from his heavy grief over the loss of his wife the year before to cancer. These guys were his best friends from way back when he had been known as "Little Dickie," before his massive growth spurt and dedication to the gym. These were the buddies who had defended him when he had been the smallest guy on their intramural hockey team and had spent more time getting body checked into the wall than using his stick. Literally and figuratively.

He'd do anything to help any one of them, and right now, Sullivan needed a whole hell of a lot of help. He had been drowning in guilt and grief in the ten months since Kendra had died. "I'm in. I'll dance all night for a good cause. Especially if I can wear a banana hammock. What man doesn't want to strut on stage in some tight-ass underwear?"

He said it solely for a reaction and he got one.

Sullivan snorted. "Me. No. I'm not doing it, Lil. Forget it. I'm a father. It's just fucking inappropriate."

"Finn is not going to be at the show," Lilly said dryly. "He's a year old. You'll have plenty of time to embarrass him in a decade, but right now he is not going to care. Trust me."

Their buddy just rolled his eyes. "Still not doing it."

"I'll do it." Axl shrugged, taking his patrolman's hat off and tossing it on the bar top. "I'd like to think we could pull in some cash making fools out of ourselves."

"You're a cop," Sullivan said, pointing out the obvious. "That's way too embarrassing. Have you lost your damn mind?"

Axl was even-tempered to the extreme. If he thought it was a good idea, Rick trusted that it was. "Have you seen the viral videos cops do now? I'm cool with anything for charity."

"Whatever, dude." Sullivan shook his head. "You're all idiots."

"When do you want to do this?" Rick asked Lilly. He'd never admit it, but he was into the whole idea. It would probably draw women in from neighboring towns and he was not a guy to turn down being objectified. He'd worked hard to have abs and he'd show them all damn day long.

"I was thinking August eighteenth-ish."

Damn. That was two days after the one year anniversary of Kendra's untimely and tragic death. The day of the funeral.

Sullivan's nostrils flared. "Fuck that. No." He made a move like he was going to leave his own bar.

Axl held his hand up. "Whoa. Calm down. So what, you're just going to stay at home and get wasted by yourself that whole week?" Axl asked, throwing it out there. "Dude, no. Let's do something ridiculous and raise some money. Kendra would have liked that."

Rick knew Axl had pushed a hot button and he waited for their friend to explode. But surprisingly, even though Sullivan's jaw worked he just reached for a bottle of whiskey and started pouring shots. "Fine. You want to make asses out of yourselves, go for it. But I'm not doing it. I have to watch the bar anyway."

Lilly eyed him, worry clearly etched on her face. Rick knew, without a doubt, that Lilly was in love with Sullivan and had been for years. She was watching him drink heavily and Rick knew it was breaking her heart. But she was smart enough not to go there with Sullivan. He wasn't ready for anyone to care about him.

She turned to Rick. "Do you think Brandon and Jesse will do it?"

Rick nodded. "Are you kidding? As long as you can work around Jesse's schedule, he'll be in. He loves the limelight." Jesse was playing pro hockey, the only one of their group of friends to really pursue the sport. For the rest of them, it had just been fun. Rick had always been more into working with his hands than going hard core on the ice, even after he grew a foot and a half and gained sixty pounds of hard-packed muscle. Brandon was living in Chicago, working in finance and was a partier, living the single life to the hilt. "Brandon is always up for a good time."

Sullivan threw back his drink, wincing at the burn. "This isn't a good time. No one should be celebrating cancer. This is stupid."

Rick and Axl both said nothing, knowing it would be Lilly who could get through to him. Lilly reached over the counter and rested her hand over top of Sullivan's. He glanced down at it like her touch offended him.

"Sullivan. Listen to me. No one is celebrating cancer or death. We want to celebrate Kendra's life. It's been a horrible year for you, for her parents. For me, her best friend. I just want people to remember her before the cancer. She was sweet and fun and cheerful and she would love this. She really would." She rubbed his hand. "Do you trust me?"

Sullivan wouldn't look at her. "Of course. That's not the issue."

Rick could see him visibly swallowing, like his emotions were crawling up his throat. He felt some serious compassion for his old friend. "Think of it as a favor to me," he told Sullivan. "If I can strut on stage I can finally put that stupid childhood nickname to rest once and for all." He put his hands up, far apart, to indicate a very large cock. "No one is going to see me in some tight boxer briefs and have the balls to call me Little Dickie ever again."

Seriously. Worst nickname ever.

It drew a snort from Sullivan. "Keep dreaming, Little Dickie."

Rick stood up and put his hand on the snap of his jeans. "You want me to prove it right now, motherfucker?"

"Yes." Sullivan crossed his arms over his chest in a blatant challenge.

Rick had no problem whipping it out. He'd spent a lifetime proving himself as the short kid from the wrong side of the tracks. He was used to backing his trash talk up with action, even if it was just getting razzed by his best friend.

"Oh, my God, no, stop!" Lilly put her hand up, her expression one of horror.

It made Rick laugh. "Are you scared you might like what you see?" he said with a grin.

"I'm sure I would be overwhelmed with lust and mouthwatering anticipation, yes," she said dryly. "That's why you need to keep it in your pants. I don't want you to see me like that, desperate for some action."

Rick sat back down, clapping her on the back. Lilly was nothing if not a good sport. Far as he knew, she wasn't dating at all and she was fantastic at being able to hang with a bunch of guys. It wasn't hard to see how Sullivan was able to obliviously take her for granted. "Maybe Sullivan was right and you need to download Tinder," he said, giving her a wink so she would know he wasn't serious.

"I will if you will."

Fuck. He'd walked right into that one. "No, thank you. I meet women the old-fashioned way. In a bar. The gym. The grocery store. Live and in person." He had to admit his vice was women. He wasn't a huge drinker. But he couldn't resist a pretty woman. Maybe because in his teen years he'd been convinced he'd never get the girl. Now that he had? He was a classic commitment-phobe who felt the need to sample every attractive and willing woman.

It was a problem.

"Hey, did Sullivan tell you who is moving back to town?" Lilly asked him, looking so sly Rick felt a flicker of concern.

He wasn't going to like what Lilly had to say.

"Who?"

"Sloane."

Yep. He didn't like that. Sloane was Sullivan's sister. Two years older than them, hotter than hell.

And the girl who had seemed to make a habit out of humiliating him in high school.

All while he had silently seethed, hating her, and himself for the fact that he had the world's biggest crush on the mean girl. He'd jerked off thinking about her more times than he cared to admit. He might have even set a world record if he had ever thought to click a counter and contact Guinness.

"Oh, yeah? What brings her back? A sale on broomsticks?" he joked.

Lilly wrinkled her nose.

"Hey." Sullivan handed him a shot. "That's my sister you're talking about."

"Yeah, I know. The stuck-up one." Responsible for the single most humiliating moment of his teen years, involving a case of mistaken identity at a party. Not that he cared anymore. He really didn't. In some ways, it was amusing now to reflect back on it. But it hadn't been at the time, and whether she even remembered it or not, Rick felt permanently connected to her by that horrible memory.

So, if he were honest with himself, he wanted to see Sloane and prove to himself she no longer held the power to make him a helpless mass of hormones the way she had back in the day. And maybe he wanted Sloane to see that he was no longer Little Dickie.

"I think Sloane has matured," Lilly said. "You'd be surprised."

"So what brings her back to Beaver Bend?"

"She has this crazy idea in her head I need help with Finn," Sullivan said. "Which I don't. I don't need her leaving her life in the city behind because she feels sorry for me."

"She's your sister," Lilly said. "She loves you and Finn. But also, she just got divorced, remember? I think she probably needed a change."

Rick had known via Sullivan she was a trophy wife to her doctor husband, who was a dozen years older than them. That she had gotten a divorce was interesting. Sullivan hadn't mentioned it. But then again, Sullivan was wrapped up in his grief these days. He hadn't been sharing much of anything. "Never turn down family offering to help, Sullivan. And I hope she's happy."

He meant it. He didn't really harbor ill will towards Sloane for what had happened when they were teens. Life moved on after high school and people changed. Grew up. Rick threw back his shot and let it burn all the way down his throat. He was grateful for the warning though. It would have sucked to have run into Sloane on the street one day. He just might still be capable of drooling over her.

Axl clapped him on the shoulder. "You're happy she's single, aren't you?"

Yes. He wouldn't mind a crack at her. One night with his teenage fantasy. But he scoffed because he'd never admit that shit out loud. "No. Of course not. I wouldn't wish divorce on anyone."

Unfortunately, his friends had known him too long.

"Stay away from my sister, asshole," Sullivan said. "She doesn't need your manwhore self messing with her head right now."

"It's not her head I want to mess with," he said, grinning.

Sullivan's nostrils flared. "Don't push me, man. I'll knock you the fuck out. That divorce did a number on her."

So she hadn't wanted the divorce. That was also interesting.

"When does she get back?" He wasn't concerned about Sullivan's threats. He wasn't really going to go there.

"Couple months. She's wrapping everything up in Minneapolis."

"Interesting," Rick said, because it was. "Does she need an apartment? I have one opening up in my building. Tell her to call my sister." The shop he owed had several apartments over it and a tenant was moving out in several weeks. He was intrigued by the idea of working with Sloane overhead. In the shower. Naked. He cleared his throat.

"Man, still crushing on the cheerleader," Axl said, lifting his eyebrows. "Dude, that's pathetic."

That was a little too close to home for Rick's comfort. But he was determined to act indifferent. "What's pathetic is how your dick is going to look up on stage next to mine."

Axl snorted.

Lilly shook her head. "I should have known I just condemned myself to two months of posturing, penis talk, and a constant need to one-up each other."

"That's what you get for being one of the guys," Sullivan said, pushing a shot glass over to Lilly.

Rick heard her sigh. But she took the shot like a champ.

He caught her eye and gave her a smile. Hey, at least they were together in their long-standing crushes on an O'Toole sibling.

. . .

TWO MONTHS Later

"Happy Birthday!" Emily said, giving Sloane a big hug. "Oh, my God, this is so much fun!"

Sloane thought fun might be overstating it just a tad. Or a lot. Like a big-ass lot.

Sure, it had all the elements of an awesome thirtieth birthday party. Male strippers, old friends, and cocktails.

Cocktails which she was sipping faster than she should be because nothing about this particular night was standard fare.

The strippers were guys she thought of more as brothers than sex symbols, and the drinks were being poured by her father. Add in that the whole strip show was for charity in memory of her sister-in-law who had passed away a year ago almost to the day, with her brother still visibly wearing his grief, and none of it felt like a celebration of the big 3-o.

What it actually felt like was the very definition of awkward.

A sad, weird little mix of shit that didn't belong together. Like her life. Like her and Tom, her newly ex-husband. And his brand-new boyfriend, Javier, who was so damn good looking it made Sloane feel even more inadequate than she already had when she learned her husband had been pretending to be straight for the entirety of their marriage. While dating Javier for the last six months of it.

Which no one here knew. Not even her father or her brother.

It was just not something she wanted to talk about. Or admit. How did you love someone for years and not notice something that fundamental about who they were?

Because she had always just wanted what she wanted.

Ever since her mother had walked out on them when she was five, she'd wanted something and she'd taken it.

She had wanted Tom, pursued him heavily, married him,

and now she had nothing. No job, no house, no husband, no dog.

That was one of the worst parts. Tom had kept her dog, Kate. She had cried and pleaded and argued with her lawyer, but Tom had bought the dog and he refused to relinquish her and it would have cost far too much to drag the divorce out. Losing Kate had possibly left a bigger hole in her heart than the end of her marriage. Actually, not *possibly*. It had. She missed her beautiful sweet Golden Retriever and how she always managed to look like she was grinning.

She did not miss Tom.

He could go fuck himself.

Or Javier.

She sighed, annoyed with herself for thinking about anything that sucked on her birthday, and sipped her mojito. "This is definitely awesome, thank you for doing this, Em. It was really sweet of you." It was. Sloane had only been back in town four days and Emily and Becca had taken up with her like high school had just ended instead of it being twelve years since grad-uation. The three amigos back together. Half of the cheer-leading squad at Beaver Bend Senior High.

Unlike when she was seventeen, and an entitled little bitch, Sloane had learned how to keep her mouth shut now and be grateful for her friends dragging her out on her birthday. Even though it was weird to see all of her little brother's friends looking so grown up. In her mind, they were still fifteen and annoying little shits who kept trying to catch glimpses of her in her bikini every summer. It had been years since she'd seen any of them. Since Sullivan's wedding to Kendra almost a full decade ago.

Her phone buzzed with a social media notification. A pic popped up of Tom and Javier kissing, looking adorable together.

Sloane wanted to die from mortification.

But then immediately felt guilty as hell to even have the flippant thought. Her sister-in-law was dead. Never to be present at something as awkward as this ever again. Awkward was alive. Awkward was nothing in the grand scheme of things. This was a picture on her phone. So what? Yes, he had cheated, which was painful. Yes, he was happier without her in his life. That stung. She hadn't even been madly or passionately in love with Tom for the last few years. Hell, maybe she never had been. But they'd had a friendship and she did miss that.

Mostly, though, she suspected it was her ego that was bruised, not her heart.

Damn it. She sipped her straw more aggressively and clicked to unfollow Tom. Moving on.

"Show time!" Becca said, pointing to the stage.

This could be interesting.

At the very least it showed promise to serve as a distraction from both her worry over her brother, and the world's oddest thirtieth birthday. Sullivan was standing on the makeshift stage with a mic in his hand. He had apparently flatly refused to participate in this strip show, for which she was highly grateful. She could live her entire life without seeing her brother dance in his underwear. But he didn't look good. There were dark shadows under his eyes and his hair was too long, his clothes unkempt. His son Finn appeared to be the only thing preventing Sullivan from losing it entirely the last few months, and even fatherhood seemed overwhelming to him at times.

A surge of emotion swelled in her chest. Moving back to her small hometown had definitely been the right thing to do. She was back home because there was nothing for her in Minneapolis post-divorce and this allowed her to help Sullivan with Finn. Her father had mentioned he was drinking a lot.

Her dad had done the same thing when her mother had left. But a year later, he'd gotten sober, gotten a bunch of tattoos, and opened this bar as some sort of ultimate FY to his ex-wife. O'Tooles didn't really deal with emotion. They were all just really content to deflect and distract.

She and Sullivan both needed a reboot in their lives, though she was ahead of him in that respect. The thought made her grin. Right. She was just winning at life right here. Not.

Scanning the right of the stage, where the "dancers" were lined up, she frowned, curious. She recognized Axl, Jesse, and Brandon. They had practically all lived at the O'Toole house in high school because Liam O'Toole was well-known for having no rules after her mother moved out. Which made their house the hangout house, with Sullivan's friends always present. But the fourth guy was a stranger to her. Tall, broad, tattooed. Muscular. Wearing a mechanic's jumpsuit and a tool belt like nobody's business.

She was surprised to feel instantly attracted to him. As in, she wouldn't mind having that much man over her. And in her. The thought was startling. She hadn't exactly been feeling sexual lately. Or sexy.

But it was like the winter of her sex life had started an instant thaw. Holy moly, the man was hot.

She leaned over and nudged Becca. "Who is that?" she asked. "The guy in the work jumpsuit."

Becca turned and gave her a long stare before she burst out laughing. "Are you serious? You don't know who that is?"

"No. I have no idea." But Becca's reaction made her frown and study him a little harder. He must have felt her eyes on him because he turned and his gaze locked with hers. She sucked in a breath. Dear God, he was sexy as hell. A strong jaw, a tidy beard, and an intensity that made her nipples instantly tighten in her cotton tank top.

Then he winked at her.

Basically, her inner thighs exploded with heat.

Forget thaw. Her girl bits had skipped spring and gone straight to scorching hot summer.

Flustered, she reached for her drink and missed, knocking it over. "Shoot!" She mopped at it with a napkin and snapped at Becca, "Well, who is it? Because I swear I've never seen that man in my life." If she had, she would remember. He was a fantasy sprung to life. He was temptation to sin like she had never sinned before. He was confirmation that lust was real and she was still capable of it.

"That's Little Dickie," Becca told her, amused, adding her own napkin to the mess on the table.

Wait a minute. Sloane froze in the act of wiping the table to turn and gape at her friend. "*What*? No way! You're just messing with me." There was not even the remotest possibility that man, that sexy as fuck man, could be Little Dickie.

"I'm not messing with you! He had a growth spurt starting his junior year that didn't stop until he was about twenty-four."

Stunned, Sloane swiveled her head to stare at him again, too shocked to even pretend not to be checking him out. "That was one hell of a growth spurt," she murmured.

Little Dickie at fifteen had been shorter than his peers. Substantially shorter. At five foot nine she had towered over him, and he had been one of the repeat culprits checking out her chest, which was at his direct eye level. He had also been, while not precisely chubby, on the softer side. Baby cheeks and a little bit of pudge that had made him endearing and cute. Certainly no muscle tone. A nice kid, who lived in a ramshackle house by the lake, a little on the silly side, and sort of the mascot little brother to everyone. He had taken a lot of crap, especially playing hockey, because of his small size, but he had always seemed to take it pretty well, with a good sense of humor. He'd had the nickname Little Dickie for as long as she could remember and it had fit.

"Little Dickie is not so little anymore," Becca replied. "And if rumors around town are true, that applies to all parts of him."

Sloane snapped her head back to Becca. "Seriously?" I mean, was it really such a stretch to imagine that enormous and muscular man standing there waiting to go on stage could be proportionate? Her mind was blown trying to juxtapose the awkward teen she had known against this mountain of a man. Late bloomer didn't even begin to describe it.

But then Sloane felt her cheeks burn as she remembered a party her senior year in high school. A dark bathroom, mistaken identity, a hot kiss, and the shocking press of a hard cock against her thigh before the humiliation she'd felt when the lights flicked on without warning.

In those days, she had not had a good sense of what would be considered big versus small when it came to male packages but she had known that she was both scared and intrigued by what she had felt rocking against her.

Then she had felt nothing but horror when she had realized she had kissed Little Dickie instead of her then boyfriend.

Apparently, the rest of him had grown into his cock. Like how boys grew up to fit their large feet and hands. He was just big now. Everywhere.

Becca nodded. "Rick, as everyone calls him now, is quite the player. Apparently, he likes to share the wealth, so to speak."

That was information she didn't even know how to process or what to do with it. It certainly had nothing to do with *her*. And yet, why was she letting her gaze drift over to him again? And why did she feel so flustered?

"Shh," Emily said, hushing them loudly. "It's starting!"

"Thank you everyone for coming," Sullivan said. "And forgive me for the mess you're about to see. Just keep in mind it's for a good cause."

Lilly was standing next to Sullivan and she rolled her eyes

at his wry tone. "Don't listen to Sullivan, ladies. This is going to be awesome. I introduce to you the very sexy, very single Tap That Dancers."

That made Sloane let out a snort. Tap That Dancers? Now that was some funny shit. The guys were being good sports about it, waving and smirking. Brandon was dressed in a tux and he blew some very suave kisses out into the audience. Axl had on stereotypical cop mirror sunglasses with his uniform and he slid them down to eye the crowd of now clapping and cat-calling women. Jesse was on the balls of his feet, like he didn't know what to do with himself while not in skates. Rick was toying with the zipper on his jumpsuit, making Sloane admittedly curious what his chest looked like under there. Among other things.

The bar was packed. Tickets for the event had sold out.

Suddenly, Sloane's birthday felt a little more intriguing than awkward.

Especially once the music started and Rick proved himself to have moves like Jagger.

Yep.

You left home for a decade and the whole world went mad.

Because, holy shit, she was hot for Little Dickie.

TWO

THE GUYS WALKED out on stage, swiveling their hips to varying degrees. Jesse was by far the most rhythm challenged, which was interesting given he was an athlete, and Sloane had to laugh as he moved like a gorilla attempting ballet. "Okay, I admit it," she said, leaning over to yell in Emily's ear over the crowd and the music. "This is highly entertaining."

"I feel super uncomfortable," Becca said. "Everyone in this room is going wild and I feel embarrassed that these women are all so clearly pining for dick."

Sloane snorted. "Do not judge the need for dick when you're getting it. I for one, recognize the same expression on my own face in the mirror."

Not that she'd been pining for dick, exactly. More like she'd forgotten how to want it. She and Tom had not had a rousing sex life. Ever. In recent years she had started to think it was her. That she just wasn't appealing, that she was too tall, too gangly. Not sexual.

It might have made her feel horrible all over again except that she knew now with total clarity that it was not her. It had been her marriage. The bad combination of the two of them.

She and Tom had been buddies and should never have married. He'd moved on. She'd hadn't. It had been nine years since she'd had sex with anyone other than Tom.

Yet one glimpse at the man on stage everyone now called Rick and she wanted sex. A lot of sex. Sex all night. Birthday sex.

The intensity of her sudden desire shocked the hell out of her.

Have another mojito, Sloane.

Apparently, she was ready to move on herself. At least with the sex part, not actual dating. She sipped her drink as the guys followed a very simple choreographed routine that involved a lot of hip thrusting and show-boating.

Without warning, she missed her sister-in-law. Sullivan could be a stuffed shirt, but Kendra was always cheerful, always up for a good time, and she would have been thrilled Sloane had moved back home. That had always been something she'd bugged Sloane about when they would chat on the phone. If she were here, she would have made this birthday extra special and would have been there for her to talk about Tom and her fear that she would have no clue how to date after all these years married. Hell, Kendra would have been setting her up with men left, right, and center. Emily and Becca had been great since she'd been back in town, but she hadn't been that close to them in recent years.

Thinking about Kendra and her brother, and her nephew growing up without his mom had her tearing up.

Damn it.

It was her birthday. Tomorrow there would be plenty of time for continuing to mourn Kendra and worrying about Sullivan and Finn. Pondering what to do with the rest of her life.

She was starting her new job at the dog grooming salon.

That would keep her busy for now and so would playing with her nephew. She needed to enjoy the moment. YOLO, bitches. Maybe she needed that on a T-shirt.

The man formerly known as Little Dickie seemed to be enjoying himself and she needed to take a cue from him. Life was to be celebrated.

Rick was owning the dance. He had an easy sense of rhythm and he moved with confidence. There was nothing of his teenage awkwardness present. The zipper on that jumpsuit had been yanked down to his navel. When he peeled off his sleeves and revealed a toned, muscular chest and biceps like etched granite, Sloane heard herself murmur out loud, "Oh, my God." She didn't mean to, but the words slipped out before she could stop them.

Turning to Emily, who was clapping and cheering, she asked her, "So what does Rick do these days? Besides share the wealth?"

Emily gave her an amused look. "Curious, huh? Hey, if you're going to jump back on the horse after your divorce this isn't a bad place to start. He owns a auto body repair shop in town."

That felt ironic. Her body could use some legit work. "I'm glad to hear he's doing well," she said, and she meant it. She may have been dismissive of Rick as a bit of a nuisance back in school, but she hadn't disliked him. Quite the contrary. He'd been like a goofy little brother. One she liked to pick on.

Then that kiss... she had mostly blocked it from her memory banks but now she couldn't shake it. In the dark, before she'd known it was him, she had been into it. Dickie had been a good kisser, which was a complete mystery. Had he been born with a gene for pleasing women?

This was all very interesting.

"Uh-huh."

"Wait. Is my apartment over his shop?" The place she had rented and just moved in to two days earlier was over an auto body shop, though she hadn't particularly paid attention to the name of it. Her focus had been that the rent was affordable and that after six p.m. no one would be making noise downstairs, presumably.

The music faded out a little and Lilly took the stage in front of them. "Okay, let's have these hot guys introduce themselves."

Jesse, unfortunately, went first and he looked about as comfortable as he had dancing. "I'm Jesse and I'm a professional hockey player."

"Don't quit your day job," Sullivan said, razzing him.

Jesse flipped him off.

"So, tell the ladies what inspires you to be romantic," Lilly asked, like it was *The Dating Game.*

"The promise of sex," Jesse said, with such naïve honesty the room exploded with laughter.

"At least he's truthful," Emily said, shrugging. She was a petite brunette, the flyer in their cheer squad because of her small size. Sloane had always envied her compact stature. She herself had been a giraffe in cheerleading terms and incapable of the serious gymnastics.

"I'm just glad I'm in a relationship," Becca said. "Because if these idiots are representative of what is out there on the market, you all are in trouble."

"They're good-looking," Emily protested.

"And they clearly know it," Sloane said. Rick had *strutted* his way to the mic. The man was obviously as in love with his adult body as Becca said the women in town were. She wrinkled her nose as he introduced himself.

"Rick, specializing in body work." He gave a sly, sexy smile.

What was super annoying was how her own stupid body reacted. She should be rolling her eyes at his cheesiness and instead she was shifting on her chair trying to remember where she had put her, ahem, personal massager in her new apartment. Buried in a box somewhere. She had yet to unpack eighty percent of her stuff, so most likely no happy ending for her tonight. Damn it.

"What is your most embarrassing moment?" Lilly asked him.

Rick appeared surprised by the question. But then he looked out into the crowd, and actually locked eyes with *her*. "Why don't you ask Sloane O'Toole? My most embarrassing moment involved her, a party I wasn't invited too, a little too much Jack Daniels, and a kiss."

Sloane was stunned. Her cheeks started to burn as everyone swiveled and looked at her. Awkward. The night just kept rolling that way.

"Damn," Becca murmured. "He's calling you out."

Rick gave her a smirk, then turned back to Lilly. "Let's just say Little Dickie was no match for the senior mean girl."

It was too much. It was the last thing she needed to hear tonight. On her birthday. When she was feeling just a tad bit vulnerable. She did not need to be called out for the fact that she had been entitled in high school, a little bit rebellious, a little bit arrogant. It was true. She'd been less than nice at times, blessed with a father who showered her with attention and gifts to make up for her mother leaving, and status in the popular crowd at school. It had given her a false sense of power that she'd had no right to wield.

She'd been horrible when her boyfriend Nick had walked into the bathroom and caught her kissing Dickie. She had screamed and protested that it was an accident, said it was completely gross, that Dickie was drunk and an idiot and had essentially tricked her. It had been her worst social nightmare and everyone had laughed about it for days. Dickie had caught a lot of heat, but she'd been too wrapped up in preserving her own relationship and her status as a popular senior to pay much attention to the fallout for him.

She had been selfish. Plain and simple.

But to have him say that over the mic, tonight of all nights?

It upset her. Irrationally so. Blindly so.

Because she was worried that she had no clue who she was anymore. She wasn't the popular girl in school. She wasn't the trophy wife. She had no career, no money, no dog. Who the hell was she? It made her feel panicky and angry and scared.

Sloane looked away from the stage, trying to avert her eyes where someone wasn't staring at her because they were liable to see she was about to melt down.

Instead, she saw Becca's boyfriend Josh had shown up and they were tenderly kissing.

Which was sweet. Becca loved Josh and from what she had seen of him, Sloane thought he was a nice guy. It didn't matter that it was a girls' night or her birthday. Sloane was not that freaking selfish. Not at her age. Not like back in the day.

But she did need some fresh air.

Jumping up, she grabbed her purse and took off for the exit. She saw her father behind the bar watching her with alarm but she just waved to him and kept going. Bursting into the parking lot, she wasn't even sure what exactly she was feeling. The summer air washed over her, warm and oppressive. Her car was right up front and she dug her keys out of her purse.

Scratch that. She knew what she was feeling.

Attracted to Rick.

And he had teased her like she had once teased him.

Which should be no big deal. Except for whatever totally mortifying reason, she couldn't take it tonight. She had dished it out back in high school and now she couldn't take it. Which made her really annoyed with herself.

Desperate to get home to her new tiny apartment and pull herself together, she put the car in reverse and took her foot off the brake. Unfortunately, what she didn't see was there a motorcycle squeezed in beside her car. There was a crash and she stomped on the brakes, her head jerking forward. "Oh, shit," she whispered. In her side mirror she could see she had knocked the bike over.

This was the most fitting ending to the strangest birthday ever.

With a sigh she turned the engine off, afraid to get out and see what damage her car had done. Biting her lip, she called her dad. He answered right away but she could barely hear him over the hooting inside the bar.

"Never mind, I'll text you." Resigned, she got out of the car and winced at the shiny, but now very much dented motorcycle.

Sloane sent her father a text.

Tell the owner of motorcycle with the license plate 162GHF to meet me in the parking lot. There's been a slight accident.

"This is so stupid," she seethed out loud. "I should have stayed home and watched Netflix."

Especially when a few minutes later the door to the bar flew open and Rick was standing there, illuminated by the parking lot lights, wearing nothing but boxer briefs and a look of alarm.

Oh. My. God. She had nailed Rick's bike.

Could this night get any worse?

She glanced at his crotch, without meaning to. She swallowed hard. That was... interesting.

When she looked up, he was watching her ogle him.

He grinned. "Is this a ploy for a private dance?"

Oh yeah. The night could absolutely get worse.

RICK WASN'T sure what prompted him to mention Sloane

over the mic, except that he wanted her attention. It was kind of a dick move, but an impulsive one, and he had really meant it to be more funny than anything else. That clearly wasn't the way she took it. He hadn't expected her to react the way she had. She'd jumped up out of her seat and fled the bar, which made him feel like total shit.

He was listening to Brandon brag about himself over the mic and debating whether he should follow Sloane and apologize when Mr. O'Toole came over and handed a note to Lilly.

She took the mic back from Brandon. "The owner of the motorcycle with the license plate 162GHF needs to go in the parking lot. There has been a slight accident."

He was so distracted thinking about Sloane it took him a second. Fuck. That was his bike. Damn it. He'd known he should have taken his truck tonight but the weather was just so gorgeous he hadn't been able to resist. Summer did not last long in Northern Minnesota. He had to take advantage of it while he could.

"That's my bike," he told Lilly, feeling a twitch in his jaw. Cars and motorcycles were his hobby and his livelihood. They were his passion and his pride. He wasn't going to like this.

"Oh, crap," was Lilly's response over the mic.

Everyone knew how he felt about his bikes.

He stormed off the stage ready to cuss out whatever drunk twenty-one-year-old had pulled out without looking and nailed his pride and joy.

Unfortunately, it wasn't a giggling co-ed.

It was Sloane, looking beautiful and annoyed.

She was standing under the sign for the bar. Spelled out over her in fluorescent lighting was Tap That. And the arrow was pointing directly to her.

Rick didn't even want to think about the irony of that and how much he absolutely would like to take Sloane to his bed for about twenty-four hours straight. Tap That? Hell, he wanted to kiss her, lick her, and then take her *hard*. Repeatedly. He wanted her to grab his tap and make it pour. Fuck and fuck she was hot.

He had a rock solid cock. And he was in his underwear. He'd shed the mechanic's jumpsuit on a dare from Axl and how here he was standing on the front walk to the bar, in fucking bare feet and tight boxer briefs. Which Sloane was staring at wide-eyed. He couldn't tell if she was blushing or if it was the artificial lighting, but she did appear flustered. Her hand fluttered up to her throat.

"Is this a ploy for a private dance?" he asked her with a grin, partly from guilt and partly from satisfaction that she seemed stunned at his physical transformation over the last decade.

"No! I didn't see your bike. You shouldn't have parked it so close to my car."

That was the worst apology ever. "I always park it there. It's my spot. Everyone knows that."

Sloane looked exasperated, her hands dropping to her hips. "How would I know that? I just moved back three days ago."

"Yeah, I heard that. Welcome back. Sorry for the divorce." The minute the words were out of his mouth he mentally kicked himself. Who the fuck said that? *Sorry for the divorce?*

But hell, he was distracted. Sloane was even more beautiful than he had remembered. In high school she had thin eyebrows and exaggerated makeup with blonde streaks in her dark hair. She'd been fond of wearing velvet track suits that had cupped her teen ass to perfection. Now she looked more natural, less *pink* in her style, wearing jeans and a tank top. Her hair was dark and wavy and her face was mostly free of makeup. Her mouth was turned down in a frown at his words.

"How do you know about my divorce?"

Lilly. Teasing him. But he didn't know if that would tick her off or not so he just shrugged. "I don't know, why wouldn't I? Guess I heard something. Probably from Sullivan. He is your brother, you know."

"Yeah. My very stubborn brother."

"Can't argue with that." Rick went over to his bike and inspected it, righting it. He loved this bike. The chrome was dented but otherwise nothing was damaged.

"It was an accident," Sloane said, begrudgingly.

"I think stubborn runs in your family," he said, standing back up. "You could maybe just admit it was your fault."

She looked outraged. "I can give you my insurance information."

"You could just apologize." Like she would never admit that before she had realized it was him in that dark bathroom, she had been just as much into the kiss as he had back in high school.

"Sorry. Like I said, it was an accident. I'll pay for the damage, seriously."

Rick studied Sloane, who looked like she had not been enjoying her evening. "You don't have to do that. I'm just going to fix it myself. I don't trust anyone else to touch it."

She was biting her lip and wrinkling her nose simultaneously. "Well, at least let me do *something*."

God if she only knew what he wanted. Watching her, nothing had changed. He still felt attracted to Sloane. She was wearing a tank top that showed off her tits in a way that made his mouth water. He wanted to tug down that neckline and suck the swell of her soft skin into his mouth while she moaned in his ear. Getting hard just thinking about it, he debated his next move. "You are divorced, right?"

"Yes." She looked bewildered by the question. "Why?"

"So that I don't have to feel like an asshole with my request."

"What request?" Sloane ran her fingers through her hair and looked at him with total suspicion.

"That you admit you liked that bathroom kiss we shared."

Her jaw dropped. "That's your request? That was twelve years ago! What difference does it make?"

Rick smiled at her. The smile he knew made women swoon.

That moment, when Sloane had been horrified to see she had been kissing him and loudly protested to everyone that she had not enjoyed it, had been a social turning point for him. He had, after the initial humiliation, gotten status with the guys as having the balls to do what he had done. Sneaking in a window and going for it when Sloane thought he was Nick. It was a bold move. One he had not regretted.

He'd spend the years immediately after studying girls and women and gauging their responses to other, more attractive guys. Then when he had started to pick up some height and muscle, he'd made it his life's mission to make women feel fantastic. For a brief moment in the store giving them a compliment, or all night long in his bed, depending on the woman. It was something of a personal calling.

Make the ladies happy.

But right now he just wanted Sloane to give him *something*.

"You told everyone at that party you would rather die than kiss me. But you were just as into it as I was, I know that for a fact. I just want you to admit it." He'd known it then. She had sighed and rubbed on him and had made sounds that indicated she was shocked by how good it all felt. He may have been inexperienced but he had read enthusiasm, no question about it.

Sloane glanced away, then said, "Look. If you really want to go there, looking back now, obviously I'm very sorry I was such a bitch about it. I just freaked out because I didn't want Nick to think I was intentionally cheating on him. I didn't mean to embarrass you and I feel really bad about that."

Fair enough. "I get that you were in a tough spot. I understood then and I do now. But that's not the point. Did you like it or not?"

"I thought you were Nick, so of course I enjoyed it."

She was still dancing around the subject. "So, you never would have kissed me?" He was pushing too much, he knew it.

"No. You were like my little brother."

"Not in my eyes. I enjoyed it." It was the truth but he also knew it would push her buttons. "And I owe you a thank you because you gave me the confidence to start dating."

She snorted. "I hear you date a lot."

Rick raised an eyebrow. Was Sloane jealous? He hoped so. "I'm very friendly."

"Well, you're welcome then." Though she looked more put out than pleased. "What were you doing in that bathroom anyway?"

"After you turned me away at the front door because I wasn't cool enough to be at your party, I climbed in the bathroom window." It had been a moment of total defiance on his part. He had figured he could sneak in and Sloane would never see him. The goal had been to take a crack at the Jack Daniels her dad had stashed in the basement bar and to creep on Sloane. He could fully admit that. He'd had a first class crush on her. It wasn't a foolproof plan but hell, he'd been fifteen and lacking in common sense.

"I didn't say you weren't cool enough to be at my party. I just said it was seniors only."

That wasn't the way he remembered it exactly, but he wasn't going to argue. "Okay, sure. I climbed in the window and I was waiting to sneak down the hallway when you came in and kissed me."

"I did not kiss you. You kissed *me*." Sloane looked outraged. She pointed her hand between his chest and hers.

Rick grinned. "Wrong. You said, and I quote, 'Lock the door and let's do it.'"

He was completely lying about that last part but her outrage was amusing. She had told him to lock the door though but there wasn't time for more before her mouth was on his and he was living out every fantasy he'd ever had.

Her eyes narrowed. "Stop messing with me. I know I did not say that. But you could have let me know I was kissing the wrong guy."

That made him scoff. "Are you insane? I was Little Dickie, the guy everyone thought of as a little brother. Do you think I was going to pass up the chance to make out with a hot cheer-leader two years older than me? But, I recognize ethically that might not have been fair to you and I apologize for that. In my defense, I was fifteen with zero chance of getting action so I wasn't thinking straight. And it was already happening before I even realized I should stop it."

"Damn right it wasn't ethical."

He grinned at her. "Yeah, but did you like it?"

"No!"

"Liar."

Sloane looked exasperated but she also looked amused. She was trying to fight a smile. "We could argue about this all night or you could take my insurance information and return to your hip thrusting on stage in the world's most narcissist act for charity."

Hip thrusting he was positive she had been watching closely. He'd felt her eyes on him all night. "Or you could kiss me now and we can lay the issue to rest once and for all."

Unfortunately, the door to the bar opened right then and a couple of women came out, giggling and chatting. They glanced over in their direction.

"Two thumbs up, Mr. Mechanic!" the one said. "Love your tool belt."

The other let out a raucous whistle.

Sloane snorted.

He was more amused than anything else. He gave a wave. "Thanks, ladies. I appreciate the love."

The one sidled up to him. She was blonde, attractive, probably a few years older than him. Around Sloane's age. She pulled out a business card and handed it to him. "If you're single and you want some company, give me a call."

He took the card and glanced down at it. Nicole Bynes. Personal Finance. "Thanks, I'll do that. Pleasure to meet you, Nicole." He reached out and shook first her hand, then her friend's. "I'm Rick."

"Liz," the friend said, a smirk playing across her lips.

"This is Sloane," he said, gesturing to where his best friend's sister was standing stone-faced and skeptical.

But Sloane did pull a smile and say, "Nice to meet you."

Nicole laughed. "Actually, we went to high school together. I was a year ahead of you. But totally not in the popular crowd. I ran with the math nerds."

"Oh wow, I didn't realize it was you, Nicole, you changed your hair color. You look great. Good to see you again."

Rick actually thought Sloane didn't remember who the woman was but she covered it pretty well.

Sloane turned to him. "So, give me your number and I'll text my insurance information to you. I'm heading home for the night."

"We just came outside for a bit of fresh air," Nicole said. "We'll leave you two to whatever." She gave Rick a smile. "Call me."

When the women retreated back into the bar, Rick turned to Sloane. "Where were we?"

"Me leaving."

With that, she burst into tears.

Oh, shit. Hell fucking no. Rick glanced around, making sure no one else was witnessing this. Had he done that? Made her cry? "Come here. What's going on?" Rick reached out and pulled Sloane into his arms.

She went willingly, draping herself over his chest and winding her arms around his waist. "I'm sorry," she said. "These are angry tears. Not at you."

"Good to know. Then what's wrong?"

"I'm just pissed that Kendra died. Like, I'm furious. Sullivan is a mess and I feel helpless and I hate feeling helpless."

His heart clenched. Everyone had liked Kendra. She had been a ray of sunshine. "You're right, it's not fair." Rick ran his hand over her back, attempting to soothe her.

"It's my birthday," she said. "I'm thirty years old today and I feel like I wasted the last decade of my life. I was so determined to leave this town and for what? I could have been here with family. Instead of chasing the idea of having a family with someone who didn't want it."

There it was. The secondary reason behind the tears. "Whoa, hold up. Don't feel guilty for making a life for yourself. You were entitled to leave if you wanted to."

"I made a stupid life, that's the problem. I was so damn arrogant. Ugh. I didn't know *anything*."

"That is the paradox of youth. We think we know everything and we don't know jack shit." Rick tried to focus on how she was feeling and not the fact that she felt amazing in his arms. Which she did. "Happy Birthday, Sloane. Maybe this next year will be better for you."

She pulled back and sniffled. Sloane had rich, expressive eyes, the color of deep murky water. The tears were still clinging to her long lashes, but she had stopped crying. "It will be. I know it will be. I'm here with my family and that's what matters."

"Exactly. Screw marriage." He meant it as a joke, but the minute he said it he realized it was probably in poor taste. Why did he keep sticking his fucking foot in his mouth with her?

She frowned at him and stepped back, out of his arms. "What do you know about marriage?"

"Nothing. Not a goddamn thing." With good reason. His parents' marriage had been a full-blown disaster. As had his father's second marriage. And his third.

She wiped her cheeks. "This is weird. I haven't seen you in ten years and I just cried all over you while you're in your underwear."

Sloane reached out and tried to dry off his chest. Her hands were lithe and warm. There weren't actually any tears on him, or if there had been they had evaporated. But he let her touch him because it felt good to have her hands on his flesh. "Don't think of this as underwear, but more like performance gear."

She let out a laugh. "Thinking of switching careers?"

"Not a snowball's chance in hell. But I am enjoying myself, I'm not going to lie." He gave her a grin. "Come back inside with me. You can sit right up front."

He laced his fingers through hers and stepped back, tugging her with him.

"I don't know." She dragged her heels. "Maybe I should just go home."

"It's your birthday. You need to celebrate." Rick was very aware, as they all were, that they were just a few days past the anniversary of Kendra's passing. He hadn't realized before today Sloane had lost her sister-in-law so close to her birthday. Plus, clearly she had some feelings about the end of her marriage. So, while he really wanted his high school fantasy of Sloane naked in his bed to come to life, it was pretty damn obvious Sloane needed a friend tonight more than she needed to satisfy his teen desire to bang a cheerleader.

Not to mention Sullivan probably would kill him. Or attempt to, anyway.

Besides, she was back home and she was living over his shop. He had all the time in the world to get to know Sloane again. A friendship with her was appealing. A naked, dirty friendship in which he made her feel helpless for all the right reasons.

No. He wasn't going to do it. He owed Sullivan his loyalty.

Unless Sloane made the first move. Then he wasn't sure he could stop himself.

"I don't know..." she repeated. She was still biting her lip and dragging her feet. She blew out a mighty sigh. "I don't feel like I would be a good time."

"You look like a good time." He grinned at her.

She rolled her eyes at him. "When did you become such a big flirt?"

"It was always there, just hidden under a layer of baby fat." There was no way he was letting her go home alone on her thirtieth birthday. "It's either come inside with me now or agree to hang out with me another day." He was confident she would either chose to go inside or argue with him, and neither was a bad option. He wanted to spark her anger, rouse a little fight in her.

It worked.

Sloane straightened up and shot him a sassy look. "Why are those my only options? Stop trying to blackmail me into doing things with you. I don't think so, Dickie. I'm not kissing you. That was such an obvious con."

That made him grin. "Pulling out the old nickname. Brutal. And after you trashed my bike. And I was only trying to settle an age-old question."

She slapped him on the arm. "I already answered your question. And I called you Dickie because that's how I know you. This whole 'grown into a hottie Rick' thing is going to take a minute to adjust to."

They both realized what she had said at the same time. Rick was now full-on grinning and Sloane was shaking her head, looking alarmed.

"You think I'm hot, huh?" he asked.

"No, no, that's not what I meant."

"So, I'm ugly?"

Her cheeks were red and she looked both irritated and amused. "Stop messing with me. I think it's safe to say we can all agree you have *grown* since high school. Becca tells me you have half the girls in town stroking your ego, among other things, so you don't need me to do the same."

Interesting. He couldn't get a read on her true feelings. If she was actually attracted to him, or if she merely thought he was *grown*. But now that Sloane had moved back to Beaver Bend, he was going to enjoy finding out. "Got it. You will not stroke me."

He meant it to be funny and she rewarded him with a genuine laugh.

"Fine. I'm going back inside. Knowing the gossip in this town if we stand out here any longer they'll have us married by fall."

That made him shudder and it was only partially exaggerated. "God. Marriage. No, thank you."

For a minute he thought she was going to say something revealing or personal. But she just shook her head. "Put some pants on, *Rick*. Seriously."

"I do my best work without my pants on."

"I'm not touching that comment."

"Anything else you want to touch?" he joked as he flexed his arm.

"No."

But he didn't believe her. Because her eyes widened as she watched his biceps tighten. Then her eyes dropped to his underwear. Rick opened the door to the bar for her. She slipped inside quickly, and he fought the urge to growl as he took in the view of her ass in tight jeans. He would give up sex for six months if he could have one night with Sloane. Put her in a cheerleading uniform and he would up the bid to twelve months celibacy.

Without warning she turned and said, "Thanks, Rick."

It kicked him in the gut for whatever reason. He felt a strange mix of emotions he couldn't explain. The landscape was unfamiliar and he didn't like it. He didn't even know what she was thanking him for. So he kept it light, because that's what he was good at. "Come on." He moved past Sloane and took her hand in his.

"What are you doing?" she asked, alarmed.

"Taking you inside. Birthday shot. We can share a car service home since my bike is busted and you should be celebrating."

"I don't know about a shot. I already had two mojitos. I'm kind of a cheap date."

"Good to know. Filing that away: Sloane can't handle her alcohol."

She slapped his arm. "That's not a flaw."

Rick pulled her across the crowded room. "Come to the bar with me, even if you don't want to drink. You only turn thirty once so you should stay for a bit, have fun."

The hooting of the crowd has slowed down substantially. The Tap That Dancers seemed to have taken a break while he was out dealing with his bike. They could wait another five minutes. It wasn't like they were real entertainment anyway.

"You're very comfortable walking around in your underwear," Sloane commented when they reached the bar and he raised his hand for Sloane's father to come over.

He looked down at her and shrugged. "I work hard to be in shape, and after a whole childhood not being comfortable in my skin, I have no issue going without a shirt. But for the record, Axl dared me to take off my jumpsuit. The plan was just to take off the sleeves and keep the pants on. But if you dare me to do something, I will do it."

Sloane gave him a smile that he hoped like hell she intended to be flirty. That's how he was chose to interpret it. "Interesting. I'll make a mental note—dare Rick to do something stupid."

That made him laugh. "Go for it."

"So you're saying at sleepovers you always chose Dare over Truth?"

"Guys don't have sleepovers. But I would have a sleepover at your house. You could dare me to do anything and I would." He smirked at her.

She slapped his arm for the second time. "You're ridiculous."

Turned on. That's what he was.

But he'd waited twelve years for a night with Sloane. He could wait until Sullivan had calmed the hell down. And until Sloane was ready to understand he was very serious about a slumber party for two involving him, her, and every sexual fantasy she'd ever had.

THREE

SLOANE BLAMED THE SHOTS.

It was the only reason she could think of to explain how she wound up on stage with Rick and the other guys dancing among their bare chests and grinding hips.

They were her old friends. Buddies. It was no big deal. Not sexual at all.

And God, it was fun. She had a buzz, but she wasn't loaded and it felt so damn good just to dance and to laugh and to let go.

When was the last time she had let go?

It was a total relief to just move her hips to the pulsing pop music and not worry about anything.

She hadn't intended to drink any more but Brandon had egged her on. Besides, she never did this. Tom hadn't liked to go out to clubs or bars and she only occasionally had a glass of wine. Being here, at Tap That, where she'd spent hours and hours as a kid when her father was the sole owner, was like coming home to a place where she was more confident. On surer footing.

It was tantalizing.

A glance over to the bar showed her father was actually

grinning in approval. He had given her a shot willingly and had kissed her cheek and said he was glad she was having fun on her birthday. He'd been worried about her, that was obvious. The last thing in the world she wanted to do was give her father more to worry about. She knew he was stressed out about Sullivan. And her, because she had said very little about the end of her marriage other than insist she was fine. Her dad was too young to have such a weariness on his face. The man wasn't even fifty yet and he had the weight of the world on him.

But, thanks to old friends, encouragement from Rick, and a little tequila, Sloane was having a great time. She genuinely was.

Jesse took her hand and spun her around. Given how uncoordinated he was, they ended up colliding into each other and Sloane laughed.

The only person who didn't seem to be amused with the evening was Sullivan. He was standing next to Lilly, arms crossed over his chest, a sour look on his face. He kept sipping off a glass of whisky, though Sloane couldn't gauge how much he'd consumed over the night. He didn't appear drunk, but he didn't appear even remotely pleased by anything that was happening.

In their youth, Sullivan had always been a jovial guy, full of practical jokes and annoying brotherly traits. Stubborn, yes. Bossy, too, especially given he was younger. But not sour. This was new. Since he'd lost Kendra. It was like he'd forgotten how to have fun. Understandable that he might be quiet, but not so... cold.

He didn't even react when Lilly lifted her mic and turned it on to give a hearty, "Happy Birthday to a Tap That family member, Sloane O'Toole! Enjoy your big 3-0, beautiful!"

Sloane blew Lilly a kiss and mouthed "thank you" to her.

She realized that if she had stayed in Minneapolis it

wouldn't have gone down this way. She didn't have a lot of close friends in the city, having spent more of her time with animals at the shelter she volunteered at than humans. Most of their circle of friends had been Tom's age, at least ten years older, with kids. She hadn't bonded with a whole lot of those women and her only real friend had been her next-door neighbor.

This was not what she would consider an ideal birthday, but the amusing reality was that aside from Becca and Emily, Little Dickie was the bright spot. He was the same as he'd been in school in that he was nice, attentive, easy-going. But unlike then, Rick was not sheepish now. He was fully in control and a mischievous, wicked flirt. He was dancing behind her and Sloane almost jumped out of her skin when he pinched her at her waist, just high enough as to not be dirty, but still intimately. She turned and opened her eyes wide in question.

"What are you doing?" she yelled over the music.

"A pinch to grow an inch," he said.

"I don't need any help, thanks. I'm almost six feet tall."

Rick's eyebrows rose. "Six feet of sexy."

Sloane rolled her eyes, even as she felt a spark deep inside her inner thighs. "I can't believe those lines work for you."

"You'd be surprised what works."

She probably wouldn't be. Rick was hot. There was no denying it. That smile was dirty and dangerous. She could see how women would be perfectly aware they were just going to be a notch on his bedpost and they would go for it anyway. Rick seemed built for casual sex. Confident, muscular. Well-endowed from what she heard and could see in his briefs.

But Sloane had been with Tom most of her adult life. She was sorely lacking in the casual sex department.

Rick might not be the man to start with. He was way out of her league in that regard.

Which was hugely ironic.

Then again, maybe he was the perfect man to start with. It wouldn't get messy or be awkward. She knew Rick and she trusted him. Word around town was he made the ladies happy. Plus, though she would never, ever admit it to him, she had enjoyed kissing him all those years ago. So much that she had gotten flustered wondering what was so different because usually Nick didn't make her feel so... warm in various places. She had gone to bed that night desperately curious to understand why Dickie's lips had done things to her Nick's never had.

So why not kiss him now?

Fresh start.

New beginning at thirty.

Let her past and present collide.

Give Rick his kiss part two and see what happened.

It was that thought that had her jumping down off the stage and heading straight to the table where Becca, Josh, and Emily were. Slipping into her chair, she took a sip of her cocktail. "Give me Rick's number." One of them had to have it.

"What? Why?" Becca looked horrified.

Emily grinned and pulled out her phone. "Go for it, Sloane. Time to get back on the horse."

"This might not be a good idea," Becca protested. "Are you really ready to handle a notorious manwhore?"

Sloane was determined to try. Wasn't that the point? "Please. I can handle Little Dickie. I had him wrapped around my finger in high school."

Life was too short. Kendra's death had shown her that. She'd spent a decade sleepwalking her way through her life... and for what purpose? She was done. Grab the bull by the horns and all of that.

Emily shared Rick's contact information with her. She clicked on it and typed him a new text message.

Fine, prove it. Kiss me again and let's see what happens.

Then she hit send before she could change her mind.

"Girl, you're playing with fire," Becca said, when Sloane showed her the text.

Without bothering to respond, she grabbed Becca by the arm. "Let's dance." She wasn't going to go back up on stage, but there was a dance floor in front of the stage and other women had started dancing and having fun up there. She wanted a piece of that.

An hour later she was sweaty and laughing, most of her buzz worn off. Rick hadn't replied to her text but to be fair, he was only in his mechanic's jumpsuit, half unzipped. She couldn't imagine that bulge in his pants was his phone. She hoped not anyway.

When Emily suggested it might be time to leave, Sloane was ironically resistant.

She'd just started to have cut loose and suddenly everyone wanted to abandon ship?

"You go ahead," she yelled over the music to Emily, who looked like she was exhausted. "It's still early."

"It's actually one in the morning."

Perfect. No longer her birthday. She had endured it. Moved past it. There was nothing to fear now. She was thirty and divorced and had moved back home.

"I'm not ready to go. Don't worry about it, Em. You and Becca can leave. I'll be fine. My father and my brother are here, remember?"

That seemed to reassure both of them. "Text me when you get home," Becca said. "And happy birthday again."

There were hugs and Sloane got a little gushy and teary-eyed. "I love you guys. Thank you for making my birthday special."

Emily laughed. "Wow. You are drunk."

"Nope. Not so. Not true. Hardly at all." Okay, maybe a

little, but the dancing and two glasses of water had definitely helped.

They waved and fought their way through the still-packed dance floor. The charity event had clearly been a huge success. Sullivan and her dad were planning to donate all drink sales plus the cover tickets to breast cancer research. Kendra would have thought the whole night highly entertaining and that made Sloane happy.

The night was ending way better than it had started.

It could end even better if Rick would answer her text.

Pushing her hair back off her forehead she went over to the bar and asked Sullivan for a water. "Where's Dad? I need a ride home."

He eyed her. "You'll have to wait until after we close up."

"No problem, I can wait. I'm ready to close this place down."

Sullivan managed to crack a smile. "Okay, then. I'm glad you're having a good birthday, sis. But do me a favor."

"What's that?"

He shook his head. "Don't have sex with Rick. It's not a good move for you."

She was annoyed. Mostly because she really wanted to have sex with Rick and that her brother knew that fact was irritating. Also, because he thought he had the right to an opinion over her love life. "Who I have sex with is none of your business whatsoever."

"It's my business because I care about you, and Rick is one of my oldest friends. He's been with a lot of women. And you just lost Tom."

That made her snort. "I didn't *lose* Tom. That makes it sound like I misplaced him at Walmart. We got divorced."

"Which makes you not in a good head space right now."

"My head is fine. The divorce was a good thing. Trust me."

Because Tom had cheated on her and they had both married for the wrong reasons.

"You shouldn't be hooking up right now."

"Oh, really? Because I hear you are hooking up left, right, and center." Sloane was pissed. How dare he? Emily and Becca had given her the scoop. Sullivan's way of grieving might be the most classically male way—by dipping his wick wherever, whenever in some messed up quest to forget his reality.

Sullivan threw down the rag he's been holding. "That's none of your business."

Had he really just said that? Sloane felt like her head might explode. Siblings were so annoying. "Precisely! Have I said one freaking word to you about it? No. So stay out of my bed and I'll stay out of yours." She was annoyed that he couldn't just be chill on her birthday. "And forget about me waiting for Dad. I'll take a car service, Sullivan Double Standards O'Toole."

"Sloane."

With that she whirled around and found her face to face with Rick. "Did you want to share a ride?" he asked. He was back in his jumpsuit and it was fully zipped up now. He looked like he was ready to leave.

Her insides fluttered, just a little bit. Damn, he was sexy. Perfect plan. "Sure. Thanks, Rick. Are you leaving now?"

"Yep. Just need to close out my tab. Sullivan, what's the damage?"

"It's on the house," Sullivan said. "For being willing to make such a giant ass out of yourself for Lilly's crazy idea."

"Thanks, bro. I actually had fun, not going to lie." He gave Sloane a smile. "If it wasn't for tonight I wouldn't know my moves have moves."

That made her laugh. "You are unbelievable. I'm going to grab my purse. I left it on the table."

"Don't touch my sister," Sullivan told Rick, without even

waiting for her to be out of earshot. "Seriously, dude. Don't even think about it."

"Sullivan!" Sloane wanted to climb over the bar and arm wrestle him. That had solved everything when they were kids. "Stop it!"

"Your sister is a big girl," Rick said mildly. "I think it's up to her who touches her or doesn't."

Sullivan made a move like he was coming out from behind the bar.

"Knock it off!" she said, mildly alarmed. "No one is touching anyone!"

Well. She hoped there might be touching, but she didn't know truthfully where Rick stood on that subject, and Sullivan's opinion didn't matter.

She saw Lilly approaching the bar and was grateful for the distraction from her brother's sudden need to defend her virtue. He was about a decade too late on that. Besides, she had a feeling it was more of a selfish thing than concern for her. He didn't want her hooking up with *his* friend. If it was some random guy she suspected he wouldn't care nearly as much. "Lilly, you need a ride? Rick and I are sharing an Uber."

"Lilly doesn't need a ride," Sullivan said. "I always drive her home."

Geez Louise, Sullivan was being a jerk tonight.

"Lilly doesn't need you to speak for her." Sloane would give him a pass due to the circumstances of the night, but that didn't mean she was going to let him bully Lilly.

"Actually, yes, I'd love to go with you guys. I'm beat." She gave Sloane a rueful look. "Herding these guys was no easy task."

"Hey. I take exception at that," Rick said, though he didn't sound even remotely offended.

"I'll take you home, Lilly," Sullivan said, his tone hard.

Sloane sighed. Either Sullivan was drunk, just better at hiding it than she was, or he was in a really bad place. She was going to text their father that he needed to drive Sullivan home. Or maybe, she needed to go home with him. Maybe he needed to talk, to vent, to yell. "Sullivan, relax. Do you want me to wait and hang out with you? We can talk about... stuff. Or whatever."

Damn, that sounded awkward. But they were not a feelings family. They avoided emotion like the plague, always had since her mother had died. They joked, they picked on each other, they exploded. Then pretended it hadn't happened. It was their dad's coping mechanism and they had picked it up right along with him.

She wasn't surprised when Sullivan snorted. "Do I look like I want to talk? Do you want to talk?"

She thought about her reaction when he had tried to bring up Tom and winced. Yeah. O'Tooles didn't do feelings.

"I thought so." He turned to Lilly. "Do you want a ride or not?"

Lilly's cheeks were flushed. "No thanks. I appreciate it, but I'm tired."

"Whatever then." He stomped off.

Like actually stomped off. "What the hell was that?" Sloane murmured. She'd seen him the last few days and while grumpy as hell he hadn't been this aggressive. Though she knew this night had to have kicked up some bad feelings.

Lilly looked embarrassed. "I shouldn't have pushed this charity event. I think it was too much, too soon."

"I don't know," Rick said. "He could have said no to the whole thing and he didn't. He'll be okay. He just needs to be a dick sometimes when he's upset."

That made Sloane roll her eyes hard. "Nice excuse aka justification."

Rick just shrugged. "I am a sympathetic guy, what can I say?"

Sloane eyed Rick, curious and a little amused. She could see shades of Little Dickie still in him. The nice guy. The easy temperament.

"Okay, who's calling a car? I think the party is over." She was ready to leave whatever the hell that had been with her brother behind at the bar. He had every reason to be a buzzkill and he was certainly taking advantage of that but it was the wee hours of her birthday. She wanted to forget, not worry about Sullivan.

"On it," Rick said, pulling out his phone.

Sloane realized instantly there was no way he either hadn't seen her text earlier or wasn't seeing it now. It would be right on his screen, screaming out to him that she wanted to kiss him. But he just glanced at his phone before swiping the screen and opening the app.

"We're waiting for a black Toyota Camry."

They went outside to wait and Sloane studiously ignored both Rick's bike and the man himself. She would have to call her insurance the next day, despite what he had said earlier. But the real cause for her awkwardness was he was not saying a damn word about her text. Had she forgotten how to read signals from single guys? No. That was stupid. He had asked her to hang out. Teased her about a sleepover. The kiss.

She refused to regret her impulsive action.

Lilly jumped into the front passenger seat, which left Sloane climbing into the back seat with Rick. He smiled at her and reached over and gave her knee a squeeze. She didn't know how to interpret that. That was a promising sign, right? She'd been out of the flirting game for a long time.

As far as she was concerned the ball was in Rick's court because she'd thrown it out there. She kind of hated that though. She'd always gone after what she had wanted and now she was being so tentative. Ugh.

Ignoring Rick while she tried to find her mojo, she asked Lilly, "Where do you live? I'm in the apartments on Main over the pet grooming salon and the auto shop." Which reminded her. That had to be Rick's shop. How many auto body shops were there in Beaver Bend? It was directly underneath her, in the same building. He would be working there while she would be working at the pet salon right next door. The thought made her more excited than it should. Honestly, she hadn't been this excited since Netflix started dropping full seasons of hit shows at once.

"Oh, God, I'm way out in the boonies," Lilly said. "We should drop you and Rick off first then."

"Where do you live?" she asked Rick.

"Really close to you."

That meant she was likely to be running into him all over town on a regular basis. She wasn't sure if that was a good or a bad thing. She was leaning toward good.

"How cool," Lilly said. "You can borrow a cup of sugar whenever." She rattled off her address to the driver.

"Lilly, we'll ride out with you," Rick said in a firm voice.

He gave Sloane a look that she interpreted to mean that he wasn't cool with Lilly riding out into the country at night with a total stranger, hired car service or not. Sloane had to agree. "Exactly."

Except that it was a long ride and Rick's hand was back on her knee. Like a big torturous oddity that was both disconcerting and arousing. He had very large hands. The weight wasn't light. It was solid, heavy. Manly. What could he do with those hands?

Sloane wanted desperately to squirm but at the same time wanted to be so damn cool that she gave the appearance of being completely unaffected. Nor did she want Lilly to have any sort of opinion about it, either positive or negative. Lilly was chatting away about the upcoming Fish Festival, a Beaver Bend tradition in late August. Sloane had always thought everything "small town" was so cheesy. Funny what a few years could do to change your perspective.

Rick was moving his thumb up and down in what was now a caress of her thigh, just above the knee in a way that made her all too aware of how long it had been since her thigh had been touched. Or anything north of her knees. Or any of her. Rick's hand was callused from his career choice and it created a hot friction. Back and forth he stroked her in a way that made her want to moan out loud. She could hardly concentrate on Lilly's conversation.

The second Lilly got out of the car and they watched her go into her ranch house, Sloane turned to Rick. He was driving her crazy and she couldn't keep quiet another minute. "Are you scared of the dark?"

He looked genuinely confused. "What? No. Why?"

"Because you seem like you're scared and need to hold on to something." She looked pointedly at his hand on her leg.

Rick laughed and it was a low, seductive sound that made her shiver. "Trust me. I'm not touching you because I'm afraid. And I'm pretty damn sure you know that." He leaned closer to her, his shoulder brushing hers. "Hey, Sloane?"

Her mouth went dry. She was very aware of the driver in the front seat, a seemingly nice man in his fifties who was studiously ignoring them. "Yes?"

Rick was eyeing her intently, his gaze dropping down to her lips.

His jaw was chiseled, his brow strong. His eyes, which she had never once made note of in high school, were an intriguing green. He leaned in even closer so that his breath tickled her cheek. Sloane shivered.

Rick murmured in her ear. "I'm going to prove it to you so long and sexy and hot that you won't have any doubts."

Wow. Her nipples instantly went hard and she pulled in a deep breath. She knew what he meant. "Oh, really?" she asked. "And when is this going to happen?" Her whole body felt warm, liquid, and it wasn't the tequila. It was anticipation and desire.

"As soon as we get to your place."

Yep. There it was. She cheered herself for sending that text. She wanted to kiss Little Dickie. The irony of that was not lost on her. She pulled back slightly so she could give him a smile. It had been a long time since she'd felt this sassy. It was welcoming an old friend back home. "Are we taking bets? Vegas odds?"

The corner of his mouth turned up. "What's the fun in betting on a sure thing?"

Oh, he was smooth. She'd give him that.

He jerked his thumb behind him. "And look, we're here."

It almost felt prophetic. "Yes. We are."

FOUR

RICK NEVER TOOK anything for granted. Growing up the way he had, he appreciated everything positive that came his way. He was sitting in the backseat of a car and Sloane O'Toole was inviting him to prove himself.

It was his fantasy sprung to life and he was going to make her so very pleased she had sent him that text.

The text he was going to screen shot and save as a trophy.

He reached out and ran his thumb over her full bottom lip. He wanted to kiss her, but he was patient. It could wait until they were alone. Hell, he'd waited over a dozen years for this. "Let me get the door."

He opened the car and got out. He thanked the driver as Sloane slid out the same door he had exited. Her long legs in those tight jeans were an amazing thing. He felt a hint of guilt over Sullivan. They'd been best friends a long time and Sullivan clearly did not want him hooking up with Sloane. But hell, he was twenty-eight and Sloane was thirty. A grown-ass woman. She could do what she wanted.

Sullivan wasn't thinking right, anyway. He was drinking and fucking his way through Beaver Bend, angry at the world.

Maybe it was as simple as he didn't want anyone else having fun right now. Besides, what he didn't know wouldn't hurt him.

And maybe this kiss would go nowhere. Maybe it would be a pleasant kiss that would end there. But he had spent his adult life reading women and Sloane had made the decision to have sex with him. He could see it on her face, in her body language. It was sexual determination that if the kiss went well, she wanted him in her bed.

Which meant he was getting everything he wanted without any dating to confuse the situation. He had found that out the hard way. You take a woman out on a legitimate date, she has expectations. For obvious reasons.

This was basically the world's most perfect scenario.

Sloane. No strings attached. Perfection.

He zipped his jumpsuit up and down methodically, wanting to touch Sloane with every bone in his body but not wanting to give the neighbors a show. In a small town there was always talk. He was notorious for bed hopping. It wasn't something he was ashamed of at all. He and every woman he had been with had both been willing partners, with a mutually satisfying conclusion.

But this was different.

This was Sloane.

Which he had to admit, gave him pause even though he didn't want it to. It was perfect. But... she had been drinking and he did not want her to regret anything tomorrow. His conscience started to work on him. Damn it. He'd have to proceed with caution.

"How long are you in town for?" he asked her. "Is this a temporary thing until Sullivan regroups?" He already knew it wasn't. He'd seen the lease she had signed because his sister forwarded all electronic documents of importance to him. It had been a twelve-month lease. He wondered if Sloane knew that he owned the building and, behind the LLC name on the lease, was technically her landlord.

Sloane stopped in front of the door to the apartment building and turned to him. "I plan to stay here forever this time." She tilted her head to the sky. "God, it's beautiful out tonight, isn't it? It's the absolute perfect temperature."

"It is perfect tonight." But all he saw was her. She had grown even further into her beauty, something he couldn't have imagined at fifteen. He'd thought she was perfect then. But now she moved less self-consciously, with a simple confidence instead of the haughty veneer of her teen years. She had long cheekbones, full lips, and wide, luminous eyes the color of the lake in the summer. A deep, murky blue. She'd allowed her hair to relax in gentle raven waves now, unlike the stark, pin-straight style she'd had before. Everything about her seemed softer, gentler.

Yet that signature sassiness was still there.

"You are a shameless flirt," she told him. "But I like it. For tonight, I like it."

"Tonight is all that matters," he said, and he meant it. "Now let me kiss you under the moonlight."

"Do what you need to do." Her tongue came out and slipped over her bottom lip.

Rick fought the urge to groan. She wasn't wearing lipstick, her makeup simple and neutral. He moved in closer to her, enjoying the way her eyes widened a little. He put his hand on the door, over her head, slightly to the right. The movement brought his chest closer to hers and she pressed herself back against the steel door as he invaded her space. She was nearly his height, with him only a few inches on her. It allowed them to gaze at each other, Rick taking in every one of her features, studying her gorgeous and expressive eyes.

He had a hard cock already and he hadn't even touched her.

"I definitely need to do this," he said, and he lowered his mouth to hers.

Before his lips completely touched hers, he heard her soft sigh of pleasure and it made him even harder.

The kiss did not disappoint. It was everything he remembered, but turned up. It was an adult kiss, with all the ease and skill of his years of experience. In high school, it had been chemistry. Just raw, unexpected chemistry as their mouths had moved over each other.

Now it was everything.

Sloane leaned in to him and it was a hot, scorching kiss. A perfect fit.

With his free hand, Rick reached up to Sloane's neck and cupped her to bring her forward, even closer. He wanted their bodies brushing, touching. Her breasts teased against him as he eased his fingers into her hair at the nape of her neck. She smelled like lavender. She tasted like mint and tequila and the sugar sweetness of the syrup in her mojitos. It was amazing.

The kiss didn't end. It went on and on, pouring over them like honey out of the jar. Warm and delicious, desire rising in him with a slow simmer. It wasn't urgent or desperate, but deep and persistent.

When he finally pulled back, but staying firmly in her space, she let out an exhalation of air.

"You've been practicing that, haven't you?" she asked, teeth sinking into her bottom lip in a way that made his cock throb.

He gave her a smile. "Yes. Hours and hours of dedication."

Sloane pushed on his chest just slightly, so he shifted backward. "It paid off."

Basically, that was better than winning the lottery. But he was entertained by her reluctance to say she enjoyed it. "You're not going to admit you liked making out with me in the bathroom, are you?"

She shook her head. "No. I'm not. Save your breath."

"For what?"

Sloane didn't answer. She just dug in her purse for her keys, then turned and opened the exterior door. It was a small building, just four units total. She didn't say goodnight but she didn't invite him in either.

He got a fabulous view of her ass climbing the stairs in front of him as he stood in the open doorway, still at street level.

"What are you doing?" she asked him, glancing back at him over her shoulder.

"Waiting for you to tell me what you want from me. Send me home or invite me in, Sloane." He wasn't the guy who was going to push what he wanted. Not with any woman but definitely not with Sloane. She was his best friend's sister. He also wanted to delay the moment when she realized he lived directly across the hall from her.

Sloane looked flustered. "Oh. Wow, I suck at flirting, don't I? I'm out of practice."

"Are you flirting with me?"

She nodded, slowly. "Yes. I want you to come in, Rick."

Best thing he'd heard all night.

He took one step then he said, "Tell me this before I come up there. On a scale of one to ten, how drunk are you?" He did not want her to wake up with a pounding head and a shitload of regret.

"What is one and what is ten?" She clutched her keys and stared down at him, her hair tumbling forward, expression amused.

"One is you could walk a tightrope suspended between two skyscrapers. Ten is there is a high probability you'll end the night over the toilet and won't remember any of this tomorrow."

She cocked her head and smiled. "I think I'm a four. I couldn't walk a tightrope but I could walk a straight line. And actually even stone cold sober I couldn't walk a tightrope. Will I remember this? Yes. I can one hundred percent guarantee that."

That was very good news. He took another step up. She didn't look or sound particularly drunk so he was reassured she was in control.

"What are you on your one to ten scale?" she asked.

"A two." He hadn't drank that much and what he had, he had danced off.

"So no whiskey dick?"

That made him pause, caught off-guard. He laughed. "No whiskey dick."

"Is that really a thing?" she asked, wrinkling her nose.

Damn, she was so sexy. Rick took two more steps. "I wouldn't know. It's never been an issue for me. And with you? I can give you a one hundred percent guarantee I will be hard as a fucking rock."

Her eyes widened. "You sound very confident."

"Oh, I am." He took another step. There were eight steps in total and he was halfway to her. Halfway to the woman who had plagued his teenage dreams and had made him hard with just one kiss at the door. He felt like he was stalking her, and maybe he was. But he wanted Sloane like he'd never wanted another woman.

She pulled her phone out and started texting.

"Who the hell are you texting?" he asked. "I'm standing right here."

"Becca. I promised her I would when I got home." She tucked her phone back away and looked down at him. "Can you promise me something?" she asked.

The stair treads creaked beneath his weight. "I can't promise you I will hold back, no."

Even in the dim light of the hallway he could see her cheeks turn pink. She laughed softly. "No. I want you to promise you won't tell Sullivan. Even though it's none of his business, I don't want to upset him."

Shit. He did not want to think about Sullivan. He wasn't sure why Sullivan had been so pissed but he clearly had been. He was on the same page as Sloane and he didn't want to waste time talking about her brother. "I don't kiss and tell." He took the last two steps and cupped her cheeks with his rough palms. He kissed one corner of her mouth, then the other.

She sighed and leaned into him, her voice a soft murmur. "And this is just one night, right? It won't be weird or complicated or awkward?"

Rick wasn't one for overthinking it, but Sloane clearly was. He didn't think she'd been like that in high school but she was fresh off a divorce. It occurred to him he might be the first guy she had been with since her split and that was hot as hell.

"One night. Nothing weird or awkward." He stroked her hair back from her cheeks. He was one step below her which put them right about at eye level.

She nodded, like she was reassuring herself. "Perfect. Tonight, then we never talk about this ever again."

"If that's what you want." It was more than he had ever expected from Sloane. "So what are you doing here, work-wise?" he asked, curious. Last he'd heard, she hadn't worked in Minneapolis. Which seemed boring as fuck to him, but then again, he'd never aspired to be a trophy husband. It wasn't in his DNA. He'd been taking care of his father and his little sisters as long as he could remember, and had started working at fifteen.

But Sloane smiled at him. "Didn't I just say no small talk? I'm not here for the conversation."

Damn. "Okay, then. Understood. Use my tongue for better purposes."

Sloane gave him a look that made him want to throw her against the nearest wall. "Exactly," she said. "Let's just say I've been underserved in that capacity in recent years. If you catch my drift."

Oh, he caught it. He wasn't sure whether to punch Tom Kincaid in the fucking face for neglecting Sloane's needs or to thank him. "I'm your man," he told her, keeping his tone easy, casual.

As she opened the door to her apartment, she gave him a bemused head shake. "Never thought this would be happening. Me and Little Dickie."

He wasn't even offended by the stupid nickname. She could call him whatever the hell she wanted as long as she was naked for him. "Life takes some strange twists and turns."

"That it does." Sloane stepped inside. "Come on in."

He wasn't sure what he was expecting. But he had thought it would be put together, like Sloane herself. She'd always been the cool girl. Yet she had just moved in, so he wasn't sure why he thought she would be fully unpacked. It was a jumble of boxes and furniture. Chaotic in a way that instantly gave him a sense of claustrophobia.

He lived in defiance of the way he had grown up, with a full-blown hoarder for a father. He gave new meaning to the word minimalist. Every single item in his apartment was utilitarian. It was stark and maybe even a little cold. Except for River's room. He let her do whatever she wanted in there, which usually involved lots of stuffed animals and trinket jewelry.

"Sorry for the mess," she said. "It's been a long time since I've moved. I forgot how much work it is."

He wanted to ask her what had gone wrong in her marriage, but it was none of his damn business and he knew that. "No worries. I'm not here for the décor."

"I guess not," she said, leaning against the wall and bending down and removing her sandals.

He took that as a hint and toed off his work boots. He

followed her into the living room but then she dropped her purse on the coffee table and said, "I'll offer you a drink but I'm not going to sit here and have a conversation. I want you to just take me into the bedroom. Now."

What the hell was he supposed to say to that? Other than fuck yeah. "I can do that." That struck him more as the Sloane he remembered. She took what she wanted. "If you're sure this is what you want." Now why the fuck did he say that? God, sometimes he hated himself. He was too much of a nice guy. It might nearly kill him, but he could walk away if Sloane had any doubts.

But she shook her head. "I'm sure." She gave him a grin. "And it better not suck."

That didn't worry him. It just made him laugh. Damn, she was just as bold as he remembered. "I told you, I offer a one hundred percent satisfaction guarantee."

"I could have used that on my last car I bought. I've just never had a hookup in my life and I don't know the rules. Am I being too aggressive?" She didn't look upset. More like a little amused with herself.

That made his heart squeeze. He had never in a million years thought he would be the one reassuring Sloane. "You're not being too anything. Just be you. That's why I'm here. Because you're you." Rick took her hand and tugged her closer to him. He brushed her dark hair off her cheek and caressed her soft skin. "There are no rules. It's all about having fun, feeling good."

"Fun. What an interesting concept. I might have forgotten how to do that."

"You looked like you figured out how to on the dance floor tonight." Rick kissed the corner of her mouth. Then the other. She sighed. He ran his lips along her jawline, teasing up to her earlobe. "You're so beautiful."

"You're not so bad yourself." Her voice had softened, notched down to just above a whisper.

Rick pulled back just enough so he could cup her cheeks and give her a soft, lingering kiss. "I'm going to take you to bed now."

She nodded, clearly confident in her decision. "I'd like that."

Lowering his arms, he reached around behind her tight ass and hauled her up against him. Then he lifted her up off the ground and threw her over his shoulder. Sloane shrieked.

"What the hell? What are you doing? I'm too tall for this!"

Her hair dangled down over his back and she attempted to swat at his ass.

"You are not too tall for anything." He started walking in the direction of the bedroom. He knew the layout well since he'd owned the building for two years. Sloane felt light and leggy in his hold. It wasn't a huge effort on his part to carry her. He'd done a lot of time in the gym and Sloane was thin. "You don't want conversation. I don't want complaining."

That earned him a whack on his ass.

Rick grinned. "I would watch where you smack me if I were you. Turnabout is fair play."

She sounded more turned on than indignant. "So what does that mean? I get to throw you over my shoulder?"

That made him laugh. "If you can do that, I will sign you up for American Ninja Warrior."

With that he strode into her bedroom and dropped her sexy little ass on her bed.

She gave him a smirk. "Like I said my flirtation skills are rusty but what popped into my head is that you are a wall I'd like to climb."

Rick didn't think she'd forgotten how to drive a man crazy. "On a scale of one to ten I give you a six for that one."

"A six?" she asked, sounding indignant as she leaned back

on her elbows and tossed her hair over her shoulder. "Why? And what is with you and your one to ten scales?"

"You get a six because you're sexy as hell but that was almost as corny as my lines."

"Then we're back to no talking, you Magic Mike wannabe. So shut up and kiss me."

"I can do that."

The question was where did he kiss her first?

SLOANE COULDN'T BELIEVE Rick had been capable of carrying her like that. It was not an easy position to throw a woman into, plus she was leggy. His arm strength was seriously sexy. She had been bouncing a little, but not uncomfortably so. It was just odd, and intimate.

And yet... she liked it. It was very alpha. Very masculine. Very boy meets girl, boy wants girl. Boy captures girl.

Her marriage had been nothing like that.

So when Rick brought her down onto her bed with a slight bounce and moved over her, she felt a little shiver of anticipation. This was good stuff.

She would not call herself shy or insecure for the most part. But holy hell, it had been ten years since she'd kissed another man and that was about nine and a half years too long. Kissing Rick was eye-opening. And awe-inspiring.

Then when he'd thrown her over his shoulder?

Forget it. She had almost had an orgasm on the spot.

Manly. That's what he was and what she had been missing from her life.

When you marry your gay best friend without realizing it, the chemistry is off. To say the least.

Now in the darkened room Rick was unzipping his work uniform down to the waist. He reached over and flicked on her bedside lamp, giving her a look that made her nipples harden.

"I want to see you, Sloane."

She blinked but didn't really mind the light. It was soft, and she felt far too old to be fumbling around in the dark. She was nervous but that was just because this was impulsive and it had been so long since she'd been with another man. But not shy.

Rick was hot and she might as well enjoy the view. There was nothing of the goofy teenager left in him. He had been more than compensated for those awkward years by what God gave him later.

If he said he was God's gift to women she wasn't even sure she would argue.

"Where do you want me to kiss you?" he asked.

"I have options?" The look was heady. "Well. Let's just pick up where we left off."

Her bedroom was dark and quiet. She kept the blinds tightly closed because despite it being a small town, her apartment was in a busy area. She wasn't used to being so close to neighbors or streetlights. In Minneapolis she and Tom had bought a big house in the suburbs so her dog had room to run. Or more accurately, Tom had bought a big house.

Dang it. Now she was missing her dog all over again.

This entire night was nothing but an emotional jerk-around.

That was the last year in a nutshell.

Rick climbed onto her bed. The creaking of the mattress seemed loud in the still night air.

Just seeing him moving toward her, his chest bare, expression intense and sexual, had her nipples tightening with anticipation. She wasn't sure she'd ever experienced lust at first sight the way she had with Rick when she'd seen him on stage. Having been married for so long meant she hadn't been looking and before that, she'd been a teenager. Making out had been fun, not something that inspired a deep wet ache between her thighs.

Except when Rick had kissed her in the bathroom.

Crazy.

Now he was going to kiss her again and she shivered. Legit shivered. It was almost embarrassing.

Rick eased his hand into her hair, drawing it back away from her face. He had those rough large man hands. She'd never been touched by hands like that. It made her feel delicate, something her height didn't usually allow her to feel.

"You're so beautiful," he murmured. "I've thought so since I was twelve years old. Just gorgeous."

It wasn't a line. She had known in high school he had thought she was hot. He'd followed her around like a panting puppy, trying to get her to laugh. Maybe knowing Rick, knowing he was speaking the truth, touched her. She wasn't always great at accepting compliments—O'Tooles didn't like positive emotion any more than negative emotion—but Rick's words made her feel warm inside.

"Thanks. I think you already know what I think of you." In fact, Sloane wanted to explore that chest. The hard, muscular, golden chest. She spread her palms over his warm flesh and did just that.

"I do. You think I'm a hottie." He grinned at her.

Sloane pushed his chest. "No. I think you're obnoxious."

"Liar."

"Shut up and kiss me." Sloane wanted to have the confidence to kiss him herself. To take what she wanted. But she had been out of the game too long to have any choreography. She felt off-kilter and she wanted him to take charge.

It seemed to be all the encouragement Rick needed. He moved over the length of her body, his palm down on the mattress framing her head in on one side. He lowered his head.

She parted her lips automatically. She tried to keep her eyes open, wanting to see his eyes but when his lips touched hers her lids drifted shut without conscious thought on her part. She just wanted to feel. To experience this moment of sensual, soft touch.

He knew how to kiss.

There was no awkwardness. He was smooth, like whiskey, feathering kisses over her lips, in each corner of her mouth, then full on. It was soft, but she wouldn't call it gentle. It was seductive. A dance. His hand ran down her side and back up again, brushing against the side of her breast. Sloane heard herself gasp at that brief contact. She wanted to grab him and shake him and demand he just take her, hard. But she reminded herself in her head over and over that he knew what he was doing more than she did, so she had to let Rick do his thing. The one hundred percent satisfaction guarantee would be void if she rushed him.

When his tongue teased over her bottom lip she gave a small sigh.

Then he bit her lip. Not hard, just a playful nip and she felt it reverberate through her body. A hot sharp tingle that spread out and landed deep inside her. Nothing this small should feel this good. She wasn't sure if it was Rick or the fact that she hadn't experienced true desire in a long time.

Hell, maybe she never had.

She felt tense from anticipation and she told herself to relax, but it was just so foreign to be with someone else that she found herself pulling away and explaining. "It's been ten years since I had sex with someone new. I feel like my heart is going to tear out of my chest. I'm nervous, Rick, I can't help it. I don't want to be, but I am."

The look he gave her made her mind go blank. He was so serious, so intense. He was staring deep into her eyes like she was the only woman he'd ever seen. "Sloane. I get this is a big deal. I am humbled that you are willing to get naked with me and let me inside you. I don't take that lightly. All I ask is that you relax and tell me when you like or don't like something."

Sloane just nodded, not sure what to say. She trusted Rick. And frankly, she was glad she wasn't emotionally invested in this. Or him. She realized the pressure would be too great then, expectations too high, if she waited and dated and really fell for someone. This was getting back on the horse after you'd been thrown, but with an animal you trusted.

Rick would never hurt her. She knew that, because beneath the muscles and the grin and the big old flirt, he was still Little Dickie. A nice guy.

He kissed her again and this time she did relax. She closed her eyes and concentrated on the feel of his big, strong body over her, his mouth doing amazing things to hers. When he shifted his hand under her shirt, she didn't even flinch. As he brushed his hand over the side of her breast, shifting closer and closer to her nipple, her only thought was how enormous his hand was, not that it was unfamiliar.

He sat back and eased her shirt up over her chest and urged her, "Lift your head." He pulled the tank top off and tossed it aside.

When Rick kissed the swell of her breast over her bra Sloane gave a soft moan. Having his body over hers was such a turn on. His beard scratched her delicate skin and it reminded her how masculine he was, how he had stood on that stage half-naked with total confidence. And now he was here, with her, for the next few hours. It was amazing and crazy and when he shifted her bra down so that her nipple popped free, she arched her back in invitation without even thinking. He didn't hesitate. He covered the taut bud with his lips and drew her into his mouth.

It was such a simple thing and yet, it made every inch of her ache. Deep down in her core her body reacted instinctively. This. That's what it was saying. This was what bodies were meant to do. Touch and tease and stroke each other to pleasure. He popped her bra open and let it shift naturally as he tasted her. What intrigued Sloane was that he seemed to be enjoying it as much as she was.

"Damn, you taste so good," he said, as if he'd heard her thoughts.

Yeah, she had no idea how to respond to that. *Thanks, it's just my skin* didn't seem like a cool answer. So she kept her mouth shut and just concentrated on letting go. Letting him dictate how this went down. Then a memory popped into her head and she laughed. "Do you remember that time I was changing and the wind blew my door open and I caught you standing in the hallway staring at me in my bra?"

She'd been so ticked off though even at the time she'd realized he hadn't done it on purpose. He'd just happened to be walking past, the door creaked and he'd turned to register where the noise had come from. They'd locked eyes.

"Yes. It was over before I could even appreciate it. You threw a hairbrush at me." Rick glanced up at her. "I deserved that. And now, here we are. Never thought I'd see this day."

"Me, either." Sloane touched his shoulders, wanting to feel the warmth of his skin. "I just broke my rule about not engaging in small talk. I'm sorry. I'm just... not good at this."

Rick studied her intently. He lifted himself up and moved closer to her face, giving her a soft kiss. "Hey."

"Yes?"

He ran a callused thumb over her bottom lip. "No apologies. Seriously. Don't apologize for being you. There are no rules, Sloane. Just go with whatever feels right. There is nothing you could do that would be wrong, do you understand that?"

Her ego was dented and she was uncertain, but she also believed that Rick would never lie to her. He was an honest guy, flirt or not. She also realized it didn't really matter if he were telling the truth or not. This wasn't really about him. It was about her.

This was about her moving on with the rest of her life. This was about letting go of the past and the hurt and the doubts. It was about saying she was entitled to enjoy herself.

"I understand." Because she finally did. She owed Rick nothing. And he owed her nothing. They were just living in the moment. This skin-on-skin, pleasure-in-the-dark moment.

Rick didn't say anything. He just divested her of her bra and tossed it in the general direction he'd sent her tank top.

Happy Birthday to her.

FIVE

RICK CUPPED her breast with his big palm, kneading it rougher than she was expecting. It almost hurt, except that it didn't. Which made no sense. But all she knew was it turned her on. Big time. Man hands. Manhandled. It was hot. He swept his tongue into her mouth while he pinched her nipple between his thumb and forefinger.

They kissed for what felt like forever. No hurry. No rush to get to the "good stuff." It felt delicious. Wet and sexy and dirty. She wasn't even sure how a kiss could qualify as dirty but this one did. It made her want to rock her thighs against his and take what she wanted. She wanted him inside her already, easing this deep urgent ache.

But Rick wasn't making any move to get there fast. He did pause to take his shirt off and Sloane eagerly ran her hands over all that hardness. In her early twenties she had taken up rock climbing out of pure boredom and too much free time. Finding a grip on that gym roll was about the same as exploring Rick's chest. Except his skin was warm and he smelled like whisky and fresh summer air.

He popped open the snap on her jeans and took her zipper

down. Sloane grabbed his hand, panicking. Then she wasn't even sure why she was panicking. She released him. But it was enough that Rick paused.

"Is this okay?" he asked.

It made her feel more than turned on. She felt just a little soft inside for Rick. She hadn't been wrong. He was a good guy. "Yes, it's okay. It's more than okay."

Rick said, "You fucking got that right."

She laughed and it sounded breathless and sexy. The sound of her own voice so relaxed that she was amazed. "Kiss me again."

"You got it, beautiful."

He started at her navel, dipping his tongue inside her belly button and moving on up, teasing at her nipples. He sucked one, then the other, back and forth, making her gasp and start to squirm. He gripped both her breasts with those rough hands and shoved them together so that he could taste both at once. Sloane moaned. That was new. Not exactly innovative, and yet, no man had ever done it. She was amazed at one: how utterly lame her sex life had clearly been to this point, and two: how fantastic it felt. It was like cutting through red tape. Just suck them both at once.

"Remember when you got the senior superlative for Best Dressed?" Rick asked her.

As if she gave a shit about high school right now. "Yes," she said, breathlessly, afraid if she didn't play along he would stop doing what he was doing. "How do you even remember that? I forgot until you just mentioned it. I wasn't even that fashionable. I was the very definition of Basic Bitch."

He flicked his tongue over her nipples, his beard teasing at the tender flesh of her breasts. "I was stalking you in those days. In a non-creepy way."

That made her laugh breathlessly. "Stalking is always

creepy, Ryder. There is no non-creepy stalking. But anyway, what about my questionable and pointless in the grand scheme of things senior superlative?"

"I always thought you should get Most Beautiful."

That kind of touched her. She'd known Dickie had liked her, but not to that extent.

"And Best Tits."

And... he ruined it. But she wasn't really annoyed. She'd known that too. He'd made a part-time job out of checking out her chest. She lightly smacked the backside of his head. "Grow up."

He grinned at her over the peaks of her taut nipples. "Oh, I'm all grown up. Want to see?"

"Yes." She had to admit, she was curious. She wanted to see this infamous cock that made the women of Beaver Bend weep in gratitude. Or something like that.

"But first, you." Rick sat back and without any sort of warning, took down her jeans.

Sloane gasped. "Give a girl some notice." He'd taken her panties down too, all in one very skilled motion.

"I did. I took you to bed."

He had a point, but damn, she was very naked. "You're overdressed, which is a cruel irony. You were mostly naked all night and now you're sporting far too many clothes."

"I like to keep you guessing."

She thought he would take his pants off then but he was apparently serious because instead of shedding his jeans he bent over and kissed her clit. She gave a tiny gasp. Oh, damn. That felt like the world's biggest tease.

"Open your legs for me, Sloane. Let me see you."

"What? No." She instinctively protested. She wasn't even sure why other than it wasn't necessary and she felt oddly self-conscious. Without meaning to, she pulled her legs together even tighter, trapping his head between her thighs. Oops. She didn't mean to squeeze him like a melon. She eased up a little.

"Come on, you were a cheerleader. I know you know how to do the splits."

"That's what people do in porn. Not in real life." She was sure of it. Like, pretty sure. Not really. At all. But seriously? No. In real life, people had vanilla sex. That was the whole reason for the jokes about marriage and relationships being the death of sex.

Except this was neither. So was she supposed to throw on a short skirt and wave her pom-poms around topless? Because that shit was never going to happen. Ever.

Rick gave a laugh that was muffled by her thighs. "I didn't mean literally do the splits on my dick. It's flirting, banter. But, if you want anything good to happen to you, your legs have to open at some point. I'm just saying. I can be creative as fuck if you want, but if you ease up on the death grip your thighs have on my head, you won't regret it, I swear."

She barely heard a word past "splits on my dick." No one, in the history of life, could actually do that unless they were an aerial gymnast. "I haven't done the splits in ten years."

He shook her thighs a little with his hands. "Focus. No splits. It was me teasing you. Just relax, Sloane."

"I can't." Damn it, she was blowing this. But she felt gangly and awkward and sexually lame. She and Tom had sex every other month or so and then it had been very straight forward, routine. In and out. Literally.

"Tell me what you like."

"I don't know." She didn't. "I mean, I like my vibrator." She didn't want it to sound like she liked nothing. "I know how that, you know, works."

"How it gets you off?" Rick asked. "That's good, beautiful. Really good. Do you finger something first, get yourself wet?"

She nodded, eyes widening at the look on his face. He looked very, very turned on. She relaxed her thighs a little, reassured.

"Here, show me." Rick reached out for her hand. He cupped it and shifted back a little so there was room.

"What are you doing?"

"Show me how you get yourself off. I want to learn what you like."

There was no way. And... he guided her finger right inside her pussy. Okay, so there was a way. She moaned softly. She was damp from him sucking on her nipples.

"Like this?" He kept his grip on her, his index finger over hers, easing back out of her and swirling her slick heat over her clitoris.

She wanted to protest but at the same time realized that would be completely stupid. Instead she said, "Yes, like that." Her eyes fluttered shut, knees drifting apart.

"More in or more out?" he asked, easing her finger gently inside her again.

He didn't push the tip deep, just a brutal little tease. "Both," she breathed, raising her hips so he could take her finger deeper. She realized the irony of that. It was her finger. She could move it any time. But there was something super hot about having him control her movement.

"I get it," he said. "First more in." He pushed her finger deep inside her. "Then more out." He pulled all the way out and rolled her fingertip over her clit again.

"Yes."

He stroked in and out again and she started to breathe deeply, the desire pulling at her from deep inside. It felt so freaking good and sexy. But when he added his finger to hers, filling her with both, she gave an unexpected moan. "Oh, shit,

Rick, that feels..." She opened her eyes, wanting to see him fucking her.

"Good?" he asked, and his voice was husky, excited. "You like being finger fucked by both of us? You're really tight, Sloane."

News to her, but she wasn't going to argue. "Yes, I like it. Your finger is huge." It was. Almost as big as her first boyfriend's cock. Either that or she had been revirginized. Because he was stretching her in the most delicious way while she rocked her hips and arched her back.

She didn't mean it as any sort of invitation but Rick must have taken it that way. His free hand reached up and teased at her nipple. "Oh, shit," was her opinion on that. "Rick, I'm going to come, oh, damn." She could feel it swelling inside her, her whole body tense and ready.

He pulled their fingers out and abandoned her swollen clit too in a move that had her crying out in frustration. "What are you doing?"

"I want to taste you." He bent his head over her without further explanation and eased her apart with those big thumbs.

Then he flicked his tongue over her clit and eased down into her slit and she nearly jumped out of her skin it felt so electric. "Rick," she breathed.

"Don't come, baby, not yet. Let me play with your sweet pussy. Just a little. It tastes so good."

"I don't think I have control over that," she said, a little desperate. She meant that. Everything inside her felt like it was driving to the edge of a cliff and there was no slowing that shit down.

"Please. Let me eat your pussy." Even as he spoke, he did just that. He was stroking over her in a way that had her mind going entirely blank. "I just love your pussy. You taste amazing."

She didn't think she'd ever had a lover say pussy to her in

bed before and damn it, she liked it. Rick made it sound like she was an altar he wanted to worship at and she liked that concept. She was a woman. She had something he wanted and he should be grateful she was giving it to him. It made her feel sexy and powerful even as he destroyed her with his tongue.

"I'm going to come," she said, because this was so good and stimulating there was no stopping it. She was going to have a big, bold orgasm.

Especially when he reached up with both hands and pinched her nipples. Hard. She gasped at the sensation of heat shooting through her pussy. Then there it was. A rolling wave of ecstasy dragging her under. "Fuck," she said. "Oh, fuck."

Rick stroked and teased and pinched until she thought she might die from a heart attack. Her heart rate was through the roof and she almost forgot to breathe. When he finally pulled back a shudder rolled through her, her thighs shaking.

"Yeah?" he asked. "How was that?"

"Go team," she said, tremors in her voice. She raised her arms, which suddenly felt like they weighed seven hundred pounds, and shook them weakly like she had pom-poms. "We're number one."

Rick laughed. "Touchdown?"

She nodded. "Touchdown."

NOTHING HAD EVER BEEN as satisfying as watching Sloane explode beneath him. She had finally let go and it was a beautiful thing. Better than he could have ever imagined.

Rick shoved his pants down to his ankles and kicked them off with an urgency he'd never known. He grabbed them and patted the pocket for his wallet. "Time to try for the extra point," he told Sloane, digging out a condom and tossing the wallet on the nightstand.

"Oh, right," she said, looking limp and satiated. "But you didn't play ball in high school."

"That was then. Now I'm a fucking baller." He shoved his boxer briefs down and tore the condom open with his teeth.

Her eyes widened. "That's a five."

"What?"

"A five on your one to ten cheesiness scale."

That made him laugh softly. "Fair enough."

He went on his knees so he could sheath his rock-solid cock. Eating out Sloane had made him hard to the point of pain. He wanted her. Hell, he needed her.

"Rick?" Her jaw had dropped.

"Yeah?"

"I know I'm going to regret saying this out loud but you have a very big dick."

That made him smirk. He wasn't even going to lie. Best words ever. "Thanks. The rest of me caught up to my cock and my hands and my feet, what can I say?"

She actually swallowed visibly. "Um..."

He didn't wait for her to panic. He slid his tip over her warm heat, teasing it over her clit. She was soaking wet and he let out a soft moan. "Damn, that's a beautiful thing. You're so fucking wet for me."

She grabbed his wrists like she needed an anchor. Rick brushed her hair back off of her cheek. He felt like the luckiest bastard ever to live. How many guys got a night with their teen crush? He wanted to remember this moment, every sound, every touch, every scent. The room was sweet with her arousal and quiet except for their breathing. Lamplight softly fell over her slim body, her gorgeous tits. Her nipples were still hard and the curls between her thighs were darkened with the dewiness of his tongue and her pussy.

It was perfection.

Slowly, he eased into her, gritting his teeth from the effort to go slowly. She was so fucking tight. A hot little fist stroking his cock. "Oh, baby, that's perfect."

Her eyes were wide and she was squeezing his arms, digging her fingernails into his flesh. "Holy shit," she breathed. "I can feel you just throbbing inside me."

"Hold on to me, Sloane, because it's about to get better." He wasn't even halfway there yet. Easing in slowly, he filled her tight pussy fully, groaning as he embedded himself in her wet, welcoming body. "Damn, beautiful. Fucking amazing."

"What do you want me to do?" she asked. "Should I move my hips?"

He shook his head, touched that she looked so uncertain. "Let me do all the work. You just lay there like a goddess and take it."

"But you're not doing anything." She arched her back.

"You want me to do something?" He eased slowly, slowly back out of her.

Sloane gave a cry, nodding. "Yes."

"You want me to fuck you? Is that what you want?"

She nodded again.

"Say it. Say you want me to fuck you." He was almost fully out of her.

"Fuck me, Rick. Fuck me."

He thrust deep inside her.

She cried out. "Yes."

He pulled back. "Again?"

She was nodding rapidly. "Yes."

There was a wild eagerness in her eyes that turned him on. Damn. This was everything. He had Sloane O'Toole beneath him, his cock buried in her tight, sweet pussy, and nothing could be better than this. Nothing. He pushed deep inside her.

"Think you can take it if I go faster? I want to pound you. Is that what you want?"

Sloane was squirming beneath him, rolling her head side to side, nails clawing at him. "Yes. I want that. I want you."

That what all he needed to hear. He put his palm against the headboard and drove into her hard, finding a fast, powerful rhythm. By the third stroke she was screaming, tits bouncing as she arched her back. By the sixth stroke she was coming, chanting his name, her pussy sending a hot stream of fluid rushing over his cock. It was so amazing watching her shatter, her body so slick and warm around his that he didn't last long. He gave a few extra hard strokes, knocking her head back into the headboard, as he exploded inside her.

"Oh, fuck, Sloane. Fuck, fuck, fuck," he said, letting his eyes drift closed as he burst into the condom inside her.

She went limp, mouth open as she gasped for air. "What just happened?"

He slowed down, shuddering with the final wave of pleasure. "A whole lot of good shit, that's what just happened."

Sloane eased up on her death grip. "Why did I get so... wet?" Her cheeks were stained from pleasure, heat, and shyness.

Shyness from Sloane was not something he had ever anticipated. He pulled his cock out and lay down beside her. "What do you mean?" Did she really not know she'd had an internal orgasm? "You came, right?" He'd bet his life on it. That warm gush was a dead giveaway.

She nodded. "I don't think I've ever had an orgasm, you know..."

"From being fucked?" He felt a wave of tenderness for her. Her ex must be a shit-ass lover, damn. "How do you usually come?"

"From my vibrator." She turned to look at him with a shrug. "It's just easier that way. My ex got annoyed if it took too long so we had a routine. I would get myself prepped with my vibrator, then he did his thing, then I finished."

That made Rick want to track down her ex and punch him in the face.

"So how was this in comparison?" He knew she'd enjoyed it but he wanted her to say it.

She stared over at him, her murky eyes darker than they had been earlier. "There is no comparison. This was amazing."

He'd take that. He ran a finger down her cheek. "Good. Next time will be just as amazing."

"Next time?" she asked.

"Yes. Next time. Give me five minutes to recover."

"Five minutes? Really?" She looked astonished. "I thought it took like at least twelve hours."

For such a badass, she was very naïve when it came to sex. "Only for losers. Not for me."

"So..." Sloane bit her lip. "What the hell was that when I came? I mean, I know that sounds stupid but I think that was my first orgasm from sex, like I said."

"It's exactly what you think it is." Rick gave her a soft, sensual kiss. "Fucking hot, that's what it was."

SIX

FUCKING HOT.

Had truer words ever been spoken? Nope. Not in Sloane's lifetime.

Because what Rick had just done to her was next level. She now fully understood just what she had been missing all these years. If he could do this again in five minutes she was all on board because she needed to make up for lost time. She had to erase a decade of mediocre sex from her memory banks in one night so that she could live to bang another day.

Honestly, she felt very dramatic about the whole thing.

What a complete load of bullshit that for ten years she had condemned herself to riding a golf cart when she could have been in a sports car.

Mind blown.

"Thank you," she said, earnestly. "You've, uh, opened my eyes."

He pulled a face that she couldn't interpret. She wasn't sure if he was amused or if he was going to say something or not. Instead he kissed her, a slow, easy kiss, while he teased at her nipples with the pad of his thumb.

"Touch my cock, Sloane," he murmured.

He removed the condom and set it on the nightstand.

Touch it. Sure. She could do that. Reaching down, she lightly brushed her fingers over the smooth skin of his cock. He was only partially erect, but even so, he was impressive. Not that she'd been around a lot of naked men, but she had not been inflating his ego when she'd said he had a huge dick. It really had filled her and stretched her and damn, had it felt good.

She stroked him, squeezing the base of his shaft as she remembered what it had felt like inside her. His breathing changed, grew deeper. Her breathing changed, grew shallow.

"Yeah, baby," he murmured, his green eyes slumberous, half-closed. "Squeeze it hard. Make that cock big for you."

It was already growing, hardening. She used her other hand to explore his balls, tugging at the soft skin, learning his body. The harder she squeezed his cock, the more he seemed to like it. He wanted it rough, which she found hot. He was fully hard now and she felt a sense of accomplishment. She'd done that.

Rick pulled her leg over his so that it rested on his thigh. He reached behind with an impressive dexterity and grabbed a condom. Her heat was tantalizingly close to his cock in this position and it took everything inside her to stay put and not rock onto the tip. But she hadn't entirely lost her mind. He needed the condom on first.

She knew now to anticipate the fullness of him pushing inside her. She was still wet and ready for him and he sank into her easily. This time instead of shock, she sighed in pure satisfaction.

"You like that, beautiful?" he asked, voice low and rumbling.

Sloane stared at Rick, suddenly overcome with emotion. This was intimate. This was locking eyes with a man she'd only known as a boy, yet feeling safe with him. Their bodies were entwined as they lay on their sides, his cock sliding in and out of her with a slow, slick rhythm. His hand gripped her hip, holding her in place as he rocked into her. Her bedroom was dark and small and there was nothing but her and Rick, surrounded by moving boxes.

A sensual cocoon of skin and pleasure. Her breasts brushed against him, the friction teasing her nipples into tight peaks. She felt relaxed, open, stimulated in an easy, deep way. Her orgasm built slowly, swelling. There was a pause, then she crashed, gripping his arm and moaning softly. "Rick..." she said, and she wasn't sure why.

His nostrils flared, like her orgasm turned him on even more. "Yes, Sloane?"

Her eyes drifted shut. She couldn't take the intensity of his gaze. "I'm coming," she said, which was probably obvious but she felt she needed to let him know. He deserved all the credit for all of this.

Rick laughed softly. "Good. Ride it, baby. Enjoy it."

When she finally relaxed, fully satisfied, he slid his palm around to her ass and pumped her hard against him, upping the rhythm. Then he came with a sharp exhalation of air and her name.

"Damn." He leaned his forehead against hers and gave her a soft kiss.

Sloane had to look away. It was almost too much. Too intimate.

She felt the weight of his arm on her hip, and it felt too heavy. She rolled onto her back, breathing hard. "I need some water."

"I'll get you some in a second. Or maybe two seconds." Rick's phone started ringing, a jarring ringtone in the dark cozy room. "Fuck, who is calling me?"

He grappled around the night stand for his phone and then dropped it onto her mattress between them.

Sloane could see the image that popped up on Rick's phone screen was that of a young blonde. She couldn't be more than twenty. Instead of her given name he had her in his phone as "Brat." Except Sloane knew exactly who she was—she was the woman who had rented her the apartment. Her name was Rachel and she had been nice. Young, but nice.

Rick sighed. "I should answer this. She wouldn't be calling at this time of night unless it was important."

"Sure," Sloane said and she heard the chilliness in her own voice. Who the hell was Rachel? It didn't matter. Or it shouldn't matter. But it still annoyed her. One night, that's all she wanted and she didn't really want the real world to intrude in on that.

Apparently, Rick didn't care if she found out who Rachel was because he answered the phone on speaker, leaving it on the nightstand like he was too tired to hold it. "Yeah?" he demanded. "What do you need?"

"It's River. She's fussing and wants to come home. You know I can't deal with her like you can."

Sloane stiffened. And who was River?

"She's just pushing you, Rach. Testing boundaries. It's the middle of the night, I'm not coming to get her. I'm not even home and she needs to understand a plan is a plan and we're not all dropping everything in the middle of the night when she changes her mind."

If Rick had a daughter he and everyone else had failed to mention, Sloane wasn't sure how she felt about that. She was going to assume if Rachel was the mother they weren't together since they clearly didn't live together.

Sloane rolled onto her side so she could listen better. She murmured, "If you have to go, it's okay, I understand."

"No, it's fine," he told her in full volume.

"What's fine?" Rachel said.

"Nothing, I was talking to—"

Sloane waved her hands desperately. She didn't want anyone to find out she'd had sex with Rick because then the whole town would know and then Sullivan would have a reason to take out his anger on someone other than Death, irrational or not, and she did not want to deal with that.

"You're with who?" Rachel asked, sounding suspicious.

"A friend."

"Geez. Can you keep it in your pants for one night?" Rachel asked. "Your body count is gross."

Sloane wrinkled her nose. Wow. She was part of his "body count." What a fabulous way to think of it. Not.

"Hey, mind your own business. And it's three in the morning, I'm not giving in to River. Deal with it."

"I hate you," Rachel said. "I'm not going to get any sleep tonight because you need to prove you're not Little Dickie anymore."

"Hey. Watch it."

"Whatever."

Rick glanced over at the screen. "She hung up on me." He gave a sleepy yawn and reached for her, pulling her onto his chest.

Sloane didn't come easily, resisting.

"What's the matter?"

"Is River your daughter?" she asked, genuinely curious. She didn't necessarily mind if he had a child but she would have liked a head's up. Not that it mattered. They weren't dating. It really didn't matter at all. Except that it bothered her he hadn't mentioned it and she couldn't put her finger on why.

"Nope. River is my nine-year-old sister. I have guardianship of her and she lives with me." He gave her a long look. "I guess you really haven't kept tabs on anyone from Beaver Bend."

That made her cheeks flush. "Oh. No, I had no idea you even had a little sister." She had obviously been born after

Sloane had left for college. "Is your dad okay?" If his father had passed away and she didn't know that she was going to feel like a megabitch. To be honest, she didn't remember Rick ever mentioning his mom back when they were kids.

"My dad is okay in the sense that he is alive and healthy and living on his terms. But he's a hoarder and the house is unsafe for a kid. I've had River since she was three because Child Protective Services wanted to put her in foster care." Rick had stopped trying to pull her over to him. He looked suddenly... aloof.

"Oh." She wasn't sure what else to say. "That's really impressive of you. You're a good man."

"Thanks." Nothing else. He didn't elaborate and she wasn't sure what would be appropriate and what would come off as prying. "River doesn't respect Rachel's authority as much as she should even though she does love spending time with her."

But then because she had to know she asked, "And who is Rachel? Besides the leasing agent for this building?"

Rick snorted and rolled his eyes. "Wow. You really weren't paying any attention even when you *did* live here. Rachel is my other sister. She's eight years younger than me."

Oh, geez. Sloane wracked her brains trying to do the math and remember if she had ever been aware of Rick having siblings. "She doesn't look like you," she said, because she had no idea what else to say. Did she apologize for being self-absorbed at sixteen? She wasn't even sure if that was entirely fair. Dickie hadn't been her friend; he'd been Sullivan's.

"We have different mothers. As does River, if you're wondering." Rick propped himself up on his elbow. "It's a Ryder trait, apparently. We don't like to settle down."

It felt like an intentional warning.

Sloane was annoyed.

And she wasn't exactly sure why. "I guess you'd better run

away from me then. O'Tooles may not like to talk about our emotions but we're the opposite in terms of settling down. We hold on even when we shouldn't." Like her with Tom. Like her father and the fact that he had never dated after her mother left. Like Sullivan, still raging with anger over Kendra's death, his one and only.

But Rick look unperturbed. "You're not going to attach to me."

Sloane was flustered. Now she really didn't know what to say. "Of course I won't." She meant it lightly but it sounded totally bitchy.

Rick just laughed. "Then again. You do seem to like my cock a lot."

"Haha." Sloane rolled her eyes. She felt thrown off-balance and she didn't like the feeling. "You promised me this wouldn't get awkward and it suddenly feels exactly that."

His eyebrows shot up. "Really? I was just screwing around, Sloane. Should I leave? I don't want you uncomfortable."

"I think you should." She needed sleep. She needed his broad chest away from her. She needed to stop feeling guilty for things she had and hadn't known or done back when she was in high school.

He didn't say a word. He just sat up and swung his legs over the bed. "Okay then. I can do that." He stood up, gave a stretch, and bent over to scoop up his clothes.

Sloane got an amazing view of his tight ass and she sat up too. She wasn't even sure if she was doing the right thing but she did know she did not want to come across as petulant so she stood up and wrapped herself in the sheet. "I'll see you out." Suddenly she sounded like her divorce lawyer's secretary.

"You don't have to do that. You look very cozy and cute in bed right now." Rick grabbed his wallet and phone off her nightstand.

"Let me be a decent hostess at least." If she had learned anything in a decade as a doctor's wife, it was social graces. Besides she didn't want him leaving while she lay in bed feeling so damn vulnerable. She hated vulnerable.

Rick didn't say anything other than "Okay then." He was very agreeable, which confused her. He walked down the hall, still naked, and maneuvered around all her boxes. He added his shoes to the pile in his hand and reached for her front door.

"What are you doing?" she squawked. "You're naked!"

"I'm covering my dick, so it's all good."

He technically was with the bundle of items in his hands but his ass was still bare and he was still, you know. *Naked.*

"Just get dressed!" Was he crazy?

"It's all good." Rick shot her a grin. He kissed her cheek. "Happy Birthday, Sloane."

"Thanks." She stood in her open doorway, scandalized as he left completely naked.

Until he took three steps across the hall and opened the door catty-corner from hers. "Good night," he said, stepping into the apartment.

"You live *there*?" she asked, dumbly.

"Oh, yeah. Didn't I mention that? I own the whole building." He gave her a wink and lowered his bundle.

The last thing she saw was him and his cock both saluting her before he closed the door.

Great. Just flipping great.

So much for one night of freestyle fun with zero regrets and no complications.

Rick lived five feet away and was her landlord.

And he thought she didn't ask enough questions? Maybe he didn't offer enough information.

She closed her door and thought about his tongue sliding over her clit while she cried out in pure ecstasy. He had definitely used his tongue for a higher purpose than small talk. She really couldn't have any complaints.

Whether she could look him in the eye ever again was a whole different story.

She stomped off to bed, hoping to close her eyes on by far the weirdest yet most exciting birthday she'd ever had.

Gone to a strip show? Check.

Had sex with a younger man? Check.

Complicated the crap out of her life? Most definitely check.

SEVEN

SLOANE WOKE UP NAKED, momentarily disoriented. She wasn't used to her new apartment with its boxy rooms and low ceilings. She really needed to unpack the rest of her stuff, but not today because today was her first day at her first job in ten years. She was going to learn how to be a dog groomer, which was a temporary solution to both her financial problems and her missing her dog and animals in general. She loved anything furry on four legs.

Unfortunately, this was not the day she really wanted to be starting a new adventure. She had a slight headache from the tequila and a burning desire to poke around on social media and stalk the hell out of Rick.

Rick.

Damn, she felt her nipples tighten and her inner thighs grow warm as she remembered everything he had done to her. The man had some serious skill and she wanted to spend the entire day torturing herself with memories of it while eating ice cream and seeing if she could figure out how many other woman he'd slept with.

That was how she wanted to spend her Sunday.

Instead she was going to go downstairs and learn how to wash a dog.

"Let's do this," she told herself out loud, climbing out of bed for coffee. "You've got this."

She really didn't but it was a lie she was willing to tell herself.

There really wasn't much choice but to put one foot in front of the other and rebuild her life. Only she couldn't find the coffeepot in her disaster of a kitchen, which seemed like an ominous sign. She had boxes everywhere and very little cabinet and counter space. After resorting to licking dried grounds and chasing it with water in the hopes it would help her head, she stumbled down the hall to take a shower, which didn't help either.

Fortunately, the groomer's shop was right downstairs on the street level floor of the apartment building. So after dressing in jeans and a T-shirt Sloane pulled on sneakers and opened the door to her apartment. There were flowers on the floor with a note. Not flowers from a florist, tidy and crisp and beautiful. But a somewhat wilted bunch of purple wildflowers she couldn't identify. Gardening had never been her thing.

Bending over to pick them up made her head feel like all its contents were pushing against a brick wall with a ten-ton force. Afraid it all might explode, she stood back up quickly. Too quickly. She saw spots and went dizzy. Her stomach churned. "Oh, dang," she murmured out loud.

It had been a long time since she'd been hungover and she remembered now why it sucked.

Holding onto her doorframe she plucked the note out with trembling fingers. The slight shake was either from lack of coffee, lack of sleep, or post-drinking dehydration. Or all of the above. Either way it was a visible reminder she was a mess.

The note said, 30 *looks good on you. Thanks for a fun night. Rick.*

It was sweet. Yet she had no clue what that meant. Was it customary to leave a floral offering after a hookup? She couldn't even ask her friends because she wasn't sure she wanted any of them to know about her and Rick and their naked tango. She glanced over at his apartment door. Behind that door he was probably sleeping. Naked. He was very comfortable naked, which she did appreciate.

How had she not known Rachel was his sister?

She was a self-absorbed idiot. If she had known, she might not have wanted this apartment.

But then again, the price was right and it was very convenient to the groomer's. What difference did it make if Rick lived across the hall?

Other than it was weird he was her landlord. And probably would be bringing a parade of women home with him since according to Rachel his "body count was gross." Did that matter? It shouldn't. She'd been warned. But it was one thing to know it in theory but another to see it happening. God, she hoped the walls were as thick as the Great Wall of China. She didn't need to hear any wallbanging.

After dropping the flowers back in her kitchen, she crept down the steps like a cat burglar, not wanting any of them to creak and a naked Rick to pop out of his apartment.

She wondered who the other two neighbors were and if they were the kind to read the card on a bouquet of flowers left on someone's doorstep.

When she got downstairs she winced at the bright morning sun and quickly shielded her eyes before taking the five steps down the sidewalk to Paws and Effect. Winnie Schwartz, the owner of the pet salon, and younger than Sloane, not that she was counting, was leaning against the reception desk and swearing softly at the coffeemaker.

"Why isn't this damn thing working?" she asked.

Her words shattered Sloane's soul. No coffee here either. This was not good. "Good morning," she said, trying to drag up a smile from the depths of her cheerful reserve.

"Hey," Winnie said, turning and waving. "Oh, God, you look how I feel. I saw you at Tap That last night. Happy Birthday, by the way. I take it you had a good time?"

Sloane nodded, praying she was too old to blush. "I did, thanks. The charity event seemed to be a success and I haven't danced like that since college." Or had sex like that. Ever.

Winnie laughed. She was a thin brunette with big brown eyes. Sloane had immediately liked her when she had interviewed for the job. This morning she too was dressed in jeans and a Paws and Effect T-shirt, her hair scraped back in a ponytail. "I didn't go to college, but I have to say I've never seen that many screaming women in one place in Beaver Bend in my life. I can admit to some screaming myself, but I am sticking to my story—the tequila made me do it."

"That's my story too." Which was a total lie. She would have invited Rick into her place stone-cold sober. She had needed to pop the seal on divorce sex and he had been the right choice. She wasn't sure she could stick to their "no awkwardness" pact though. She felt pretty damn awkward.

"I have a headache and I can't get this damn coffeemaker to work. I think it's God's way of punishing me for objectifying men." Winnie hit the button a few more times and nothing happened. "Can you do me a favor?"

"Sure." Sloane wiped her palms on the front of her jeans. She was nervous about this job. She hadn't worked in ten years and she was equal parts excited and terrified. Which was nuts, because she had volunteered at the animal shelter twenty hours a week in Minneapolis. How was this any different?

"Can you go next door and grab us two cups of coffee from Rick? He always has a pot on."

Sloane froze. "From Rick?" she parroted.

"Yes, at the auto body shop next door."

That's what she thought she'd meant. There couldn't be two Ricks with shops in this building. Damn it. "I can go to a coffeeshop if you want. It will probably taste better."

"Nah, that's too much work. Plus this will be faster."

"Okay, sure, be right back." It wasn't like she was nervous to see Rick. Because she wasn't. Not much anyway. She had just assumed he would still be sleeping. But he clearly wasn't and now she was nervous. He'd gone places on her body no other man had. He'd been all Christopher Columbus in there, exploring uncharted regions with his tongue and now she couldn't think about it without feeling warm in all those now-mapped areas.

The front door to the auto shop was locked so she went around the side of the building to the open garage. "Hello?" she called, not wanting to startle anyone. She had no idea how many employees Rick had, if any. Maybe it was a random mechanic there, not him.

She could hear banging around and the sounds of classic rock pouring out from the back of the garage.

"Who are you?"

Sloane jumped and put her hand on her chest. She turned to see a young girl sitting on a bench in the sun reading a Harry Potter book. "I'm Sloane. I work at the groomer's. What's your name?"

"River."

Ah, so this was Rick's little sister. It was hard to see any sort of resemblance other than she had the same caramel colored hair as him. She was slight with narrow cheekbones and a high forehead. Her eyes were darker than Rick's, her expression more shrewd. She was wearing denim shorts and a T-shirt that said, *Books turn Muggles into Wizards*.

Sloane smiled. "Nice to meet you, River. Do you know where your brother is? I need to beg him for a cup of coffee."

River just eyed her for a long enough pause that Sloane raised her eyebrows. So the kid didn't want to talk. "Sorry, I didn't mean to interrupt your reading. I'll go see if I can find him."

But River sighed and snapped her book shut. "I'll take you to him." She stood up. "You're not one of his girlfriends, are you?"

The disdain in her voice made it clear of her opinion of said "girlfriends."

"Nope," Sloane said. "I am not his girlfriend." She might still have the scent of him on her sheets, and his beard burn on her inner thighs, but she was not his girlfriend. "My brother is Sullivan O'Toole, so I've known your brother since he was your age."

"Oh." That seemed to appease her. She walked into the garage and glanced at Sloane over her shoulder. "I've never seen you at Winnie's pet salon. Are you a new hire?"

The fact that a nine-year-old said "new hire" was kind of amusing. "Yes, I am. I just moved back to Beaver Bend from Minneapolis. I moved in across the hall from you."

"Gross. Why would you move back? I can't wait to leave here. I'm moving to Chicago for college and I'm *never* coming back here."

Geez. River sounded like her at that age. "I said the same thing. But I missed my dad and my brother and my baby nephew."

"That's what FaceTime is for," River said.

That made Sloane laugh. "Sounds like you have a plan." Then her laughter died on her lips when she saw Rick. He was wearing jeans and a black T-shirt and he was bent over removing the chrome on the side of a motorcycle. The one she had hit the night before.

"Coffee's over here," River said, pointing to a table that had a coffeepot, cups, and some bottled water sitting on it.

Rick turned and spotted her. He broke into a smile. "Sloane. Hey."

His voice was low and sexy as hell. Damn. She felt warm and girly and stupid. "Hi, Rick."

Just hours earlier she had been screaming his name in the middle of an orgasm.

She went straight for the coffee without another word. She needed caffeine before she made a complete ass out of herself with Rick. Again. Hitting his bike had been pretty embarrassing.

"Can I have some coffee?" she asked, as she poured herself a cup and grabbed the powdered creamer.

Pour and ignore.

That's all she had to do. Pour the coffee, ignore the way he made her feel.

RICK STOOD up and eyed Sloane. He hadn't expected to see her wandering into his garage at ten in the morning. He'd thought she would still be sleeping. But here she was, looking a little sleep-deprived and asking for a coffee she already had in her hand and halfway to her lips. That seemed about right for Sloane. Take, then ask. He wished he'd had an opportunity to see some of that confidence in bed, but she'd been very submissive the night before.

The thought made his dick harden and his mouth water. He

wanted Sloane in all the ways he could have her. He'd been an idiot to think one night could be enough. They had said they wouldn't talk about what they'd done together. He didn't need to talk. He just wanted more of her.

He had no clue though what to make of her being here now, given she had basically thrown him out of her apartment after Rachel called. "You're up early," he commented.

"I got a job next door. Today is my first day. I have to get some coffee for Winnie too. Her machine is broken."

He barely heard a word she said. He was too busy staring at her ass in those jeans. He was picturing the way she had looked when he had thrust into her from behind. Damn. He needed to focus. "You're working at the pet groomer's? That sounds fun."

She nodded. "I love dogs. Well, all animals, but especially dogs."

"I remember that." The O'Toole house had always been at least three deep in dogs when they were growing up.

Sloane smiled. "My dad could never say no to me and Sullivan. Guilt pets. He wanted to make up for my mom."

Rick nodded. His father had let him have dogs too, but by the time he was ten he had given them all away to friends. Having a pet live in the squalor of their house had been too cruel. The memory wasn't something he wanted to deal with right now so he strolled over to her and poured another cup of coffee. "I'll walk you back."

"Thanks."

"River, I'll be right back."

"I'm coming with you."

"No, you're not." He wanted the opportunity to kiss Sloane, or at the very least whisper something dirty in her ear.

"Yes, I am." River was pouring a third cup of coffee and shooting him a look of defiance. He wasn't sure if the coffee was supposed to be for her or for Winnie. Probably her. He was fast learning he had about zero control over this kid. She was going to give him gray hair by thirty.

"River," he said, trying to sound as harsh as possible. Being a parent was hard as hell when you weren't actually a parent. She didn't respect him at all.

River sailed on past him, sipping the coffee and trying to pretend like she was enjoying it.

"She clearly listens well," he told Sloane. "Only female I've met I can't persuade to my way."

Sloane's eyebrows shot up as she fell in step beside him. "Oh, really?" she asked dryly. "Does that include me?"

He winked at her and leaned over to murmur in her ear, so River couldn't hear. "I got you to kiss me, didn't I? And a little bit more?"

She narrowed her eyes and tried to look annoyed but he could see the tinge of pink in her cheeks and the way she sucked in her breath at his words. He teased her hair away from her ear and gave her neck a kiss. She jerked away.

"Stop it, someone will see us."

He didn't really give a shit, but he let her move away from him. River had already rounded the corner and was walking quickly to the groomer's. She loved bugging Winnie with requests to pet the dogs. More often than not, he thought he was failing miserably with his sister, but he was trying. It was all he could do. Just keep plugging along, doing the best he could.

"Oh, thank God, there you are," Winnie said as River pushed open the door and they all invaded her pet salon. "I am dying for coffee."

Rick handed her the cup he was holding. "Knock yourself out."

"I should have poured myself two cups," Sloane said. "I'm already out."

"Then you'll fit right in around here," Winnie said with a smile. "Rick and I are coffee addicts."

"I was going to say coffee whores, but your phrase works too."

"Don't say whore in front of River," Winnie said, slapping her hands over River's ears.

River rolled her eyes. "You should hear how my dad talks. F bombs dropping like crazy. But don't worry, I'm not damaged."

Winnie sighed.

Rick shrugged. "She's an old soul. What can I say?" And he wasn't qualified to be raising her, but he loved her with all his heart. That had to count for something. "Sloane, I can get you another cup of coffee if you want."

"Thanks, that would be great."

"Even though I am in the middle of fixing my bike you nearly destroyed," he said teasingly, knowing it would set her off.

She didn't disappoint. "I did not destroy your bike! And I tried to give you my insurance information. You're the stubborn one."

"And you're so easy to get wound up." He gave her a grin when her jaw dropped. He went back to his shop and set about pouring her another coffee, whistling a random tune. He was feeling fantastic this morning. He'd gotten everything from Sloane he'd wanted and then some. She had been enthusiastic and so very easy to please.

Fuck his promise to keep it at only one night. Actually, it hadn't been a promise. Just an agreement and he wanted to renegotiate the terms. He wanted to be the guy Sloane used for sex until she felt ready to start dating again. He wanted to be her friends with benefits. Her fuck buddy. Her dirty little secret.

Everything about that idea was hot as hell to him.

Sure, she would move on and he would hate that. But all the more reason to wring every ounce of pleasure out of Sloane while he had her full attention now.

They were going to be constantly around each other. He and Winnie had a fluid work environment on the weekends because he had to bring River with him and she was always running over next door. He popped over there all the time to check on her. Plus he and Sloane lived across the hall from each other. He was going to see her around at some point even if it was in passing. There was no way he could repeatedly be exposed to her presence without at least attempting to fuck her.

Especially because right now he had no interest in any other women.

He just wanted Sloane.

Still whistling, he left his shop and his dinged up bike. It wasn't a major repair. He didn't normally work Sundays but he'd wanted to repair his bike before the work week started. He had three cars stacked up for some intensive repair work and he didn't want to fall behind. He was planning to head to the O'Toole's afterward. Though Sloane might not know it, he'd been invited to a little cookout for her birthday, something he was really looking forward to now.

He was proud of his business, of what he had built literally with his hands. He'd scrimped and saved and bought the building knowing the apartment rentals would help cover his expenses until his business took off. Now he was twenty-eight years old and doing just fine. He loved what he did and the money was good.

When he entered the groomer's he saw Sloane was being shown around the place by Winnie. Winnie's dog, Hampton, was sitting on River's lap in the reception area. She was absently stroking him with one hand, holding up her book with the other. The kid was brilliant. Rick wasn't sure where her IQ came from but if it was on her father's side, it had skipped him. He was definitely the guy who excelled at common sense and working with his hands over school work.

"Your coffee," he said, handing it to her. He brushed his fingers over hers.

"Thanks."

"Turning thirty yesterday hasn't slowed you down at all. Up so late last night, partying. Having a really, *really* good time. I'm surprised you're here looking so damn cheerful." She wasn't. She looked tired and pale and nervous. But still gorgeous.

"I'm a cheerful person," she said, shooting him a warning look, like she thought he was going to tell Winnie and River why she was thoroughly sleep deprived today. She raised her cup to her lips.

"Good. Then you'll be ready to have fun all over again tonight."

Sloane choked on her coffee, spitting half of it out on a cough. It dribbled down her chin and landed on her Paws and Effect T-shirt. "I have no idea what you're talking about," she said, cheeks turning pink.

"The cookout. At your dad's house," he said, giving her a wink. "I was invited by Liam." Her father had been like a second dad to Rick. He respected Liam a hell of a lot for holding it together after his wife left.

"Oh. Right. The cookout." She narrowed her eyes and handed him the cup with the remaining coffee. "I'm done with this, thanks." Then she murmured so no one else could hear, "I'm going to get you back for that."

"I can't wait."

EIGHT

"FINN, LOOK AT AUNT SLOANE." Sloane covered her face with her hands, on the grass at her father's house with her nephew plopped across from her. She pulled her hands away quickly. "Hi, Finnie!" He gave her a drooling smile that melted her heart.

This was what it was all about. Being part of Finn's life.

Making sure her father wasn't lonely.

Keeping an eye on Sullivan.

Not having sex with Rick.

The thought made her cheeks warm and she couldn't help but dart a glance over to the firepit where he was sitting in an Adirondack chair drinking a beer. Looking casual and cool. As if he hadn't been buried inside her the night before. She envied him his complete control over his emotions and facial expressions.

He had entered the back yard with River and had given her a wave and an easy, "Hey, Sloane," before heading right into the house to deposit a six pack in the fridge.

Finn reached for her with his plump little fingers. He touched her cheeks, squeezed his fingers into a fist, pinching her skin. "Ow," she said, pretending to be hurt. "Owie, zowie." She made a funny face and he laughed, that hearty belly baby laugh that could bring world peace if anyone ever thought to bottle it up. Forget waterboarding. They needed to make prisoners listen to baby belly laughs in a total opposite approach.

Sloane was exhausted, but she realized she was bone-deep content. She'd survived her thirtieth birthday. Had actually ended it with a bang, in the truest sense of the word. Sex with Rick had been beyond anything she had ever experienced and she realized at some point, when she was ready, she could have that in a relationship. If Rick had gotten her off, someone else could, right? In theory. It wasn't like he was a unicorn. Surely other men existed who knew how to please a woman.

It had been a long day at the groomers after a night filled more with sex than sleep, but she loved dogs so much being able to pet and cuddle them while working had refilled her well, which lately had been so damn empty.

Now she had baby Finn and her family and friends around her. Both Becca and Emily were here at her father's request to do a low-key birthday cookout, along with Sullivan's buddies and Lilly, who was everyone's friend. It warmed her heart that they still wanted to be a part of her life after all these years. A woman couldn't ask for much more.

Her eyes wandered to Rick again.

Well.

She could ask for *that* again.

She hadn't known sex could be that intense. That deep and satisfying. It had popped in and out of her head all day, making her nipples harden at totally inappropriate times. But she had shown Rick to the door and they hadn't discussed anything other than that she had demanded it wouldn't be weird or awkward.

Finn gave a happy shriek and crawled up onto her legs,

which were sprawled out in front of her. Then without warning, he reached out and squeezed her breast like he had her cheek, which he seemed to think was hilarious.

"Kid knows a good thing when he sees it," Rick said, as he moved past them, an empty beer in his hand.

"Stop it!" she said. "He's a baby." She moved Finn's surprisingly tight grip down to her stomach.

Rick didn't say anything else, he just disappeared into the house. She bounced Finn on her legs and held his little hands in her own.

The house was the one she had grown up in and she was right next to the brick patio her father had installed when she was in her teens. The firepit had been there longer and she and Sullivan also had friends over for bonfires back in the day. The house itself was a standard colonial in a suburban neighborhood, one of the few planned developments in Beaver Bend. In a way, it surprised her that her father still lived there. It wasn't really a house for a tattooed bar owner with an empty nest.

But at the same time, she knew why he didn't leave. It was the house her mother had wanted. The house that was supposed to make her happy and hadn't. It hadn't been the solution to her discontent. If anything, from what her father said, it just amplified it because then she couldn't figure out why she wasn't happy.

Then one day Sloane had gotten up and instead of her mother in the kitchen it had been her father. He had poured cereal in a bowl for her and plunked her down in front of cartoons on the TV and told her that her mother had left and wasn't coming home.

It hadn't made any sense to her then and it still didn't now. Sloane should have more memories of her mother given she was five when she left, but she really didn't. She remembered being cared for by her father while her mother was either gone or sitting talking on the cordless phone in their family room, laughing with her girlfriends. Sloane would attempt to climb on her lap and mostly get shooed away. She didn't remember her mother being cruel to her, just disinterested.

But even though she barely remembered her, sometimes she wondered if she was a lot like her mother. Take what you want. Attempt to twist it to what you want it to be. There was something similar to that in her marriage to Tom. But Sloane hadn't, and never would, just roll out on of her family's life. Ill-suited or not, she'd been committed to Tom, and if she ever got married again and had kids, she'd be the same way.

She felt Rick's presence and knew it was him before she even saw him drop down onto the grass beside her. Funny how after just a few hours she could recognize his movements, his presence, his smell. But it had been a very intimate few hours. She glanced over at him and raised an eyebrow in question.

He was holding his beer by the neck of the bottle and he raised it to his lips and took a sip. Then he said, "You look tired."

Sloane rolled her eyes. "I think you're renowned flirting skills are slipping. No woman wants to hear she looks tired."

His eyebrows shot up. "I meant it as concern."

"I'm fine," she said, and it sounded more snappish than she really intended. "It was just a long day. But I am positive I'm really going to love this job. It's a good fit for me."

"You love animals, huh?"

"Yep." Sloane pulled Finn forward and blew a raspberry on his chubby cheek. He shrieked in delight. "I have a dog but I lost her in the divorce. It's honestly the worst thing that's happened to me as an adult. Worse than the marriage ending."

"You had a custody fight for your dog? Damn, that sucks."

She nodded. "You know how they swear that you'll see someone's true colors in a divorce? But everyone insists their own divorce will be amiable? Well, Tom turned out to be a p-r-ic-k." She spelled it out since Finn was on her lap. "He doesn't even like Kate, but he bought her so he kept her. It was mostly a way to hurt me, nothing more."

"Because you broke his heart?" Rick asked, picking at the label on the bottle. He had one leg up and a forearm resting on his knee.

Sloane wanted to reach over and run her fingers over his beard and kiss him full on the lips. He was so damn sexy and masculine. Even sitting this close to him did strange things to her insides. He was wearing the jeans and T-shirt he'd had on earlier. The one thing about northern Minnesota was it was full on August and it wasn't even that hot. No one needed to be wearing shorts. But Rick had changed his work boots for sandals.

His words made her wrinkle her nose. "I did not break Tom's heart. In fact, he actually left me." She shot a quick glance in Rick's direction. "For a guy he'd been dating secretly for a while."

"Shut the hell up." Rick looked as astonished as she probably had the day Tom had told her.

"Yep. So, there you have it." She gave a laugh. "And I haven't told a single person in Beaver Bend the whole truth either, until just now. I don't like to talk about it. I have no idea why I just told you that."

"It does explain a few things." Rick reached out and put his hand on her neck, massaging it. "No wonder your marriage was a total dud in the sack."

"Rick, you shouldn't do that. Secret, remember?" His hand on her in front of everyone made her extremely uncomfortable. "Very true," she said, and scrambled to her feet with Finn in her arms. "Where's River?" she asked, partly to change the subject, but mostly out of curiosity. "Your sister seems like a bright kid."

"She's an evil genius," Rick said ruefully, slowly rising to his feet. "And I'm not kidding. She's brilliant, top of the class. And I have no idea how to raise her. I'm stumbling around in the dark, most likely jacking her up, but what else am I going to do?" He blew out a deep breath.

There was a furrow in his brow that Sloane could see indicated genuine worry. "I'm sure you're doing a great job," she said. "She seems like a cool kid, and hey, aren't you and I both living proof that as long as there is an adult who loves you, you can turn out relatively normal?"

Rick grinned. "Are we normal?"

"I can't speak for you, but I'm totally normal." A little dented but for the most part, doing all right. She bounced Finn on her hip. "Hey, you're around my dad a lot, right?"

"Yes." Rick took another sip of his beer. "I have always admired Liam. He's been good to me, the ragamuffin kid coming around."

"Does he date?" She figured if anyone would know about it, it just might be Rick. Her dad kept everything from her and Sullivan—go figure-—but she worried about him. "Does he have a secret girlfriend or anything?"

"I think the key word to 'secret girlfriend' is 'secret.'" Rick shook his head. "Not that I'm aware of, but it's not like we're buddies. I'm his kid's best friend." Rick turned and glanced at her father flipping burgers on his insanely over-the-top gas and charcoal grill. "I'm sure a lot of women would go for his type though. He's what, fifty? Still young. He keeps in shape."

"Not even fifty. He's forty-eight. Back in high school I had a couple of friends who said they had crushes on him, which was horrifying at the time. But I can see it now. He's a cool guy. He should be enjoying his life more."

"Agreed. And I can't imagine not enjoying my life. I enjoy my life a lot."

Rachel's body count comment popped into Sloane's head.

She was sorry she had brought the subject of dating up. She made a face. "So I hear."

"Jealous?"

"No. And you already asked me that. Stop repeating yourself."

"You repeated yourself first," he pointed out. "You already mentioned rumor has it I'm never lonely."

He was right, which annoyed her. She had no comeback, which further annoyed her.

River came over and saved her from saying someone petty or stupid. She was tempted to give the kid five bucks for saving her ass.

"Hi, Sloane."

"Hi, River. What's up?"

"Can I hold the baby?" River had her arms outstretched.

"Sure." She passed Finn down to River, who confidently put him on her hip and started kissing the top of his head. "Cute Finn." Then she turned to her brother. "I'm a vegetarian now."

Rick groaned. "River. Where did that come from? The only food here is hot dogs and burgers."

"I'm fine. I'll eat the fruit and the chips."

If Sloane thought about it, that's really all she wanted to eat too. The kid might be on to something.

"What brought this on?"

"I watched a documentary. Don't worry, I'm working on a Power Point presentation to show you the evils of animal farming in the US and the underlying health risks."

Rick sighed and looked at Sloane. "The thing is, she means it. By tomorrow I'll be watching her presentation and resenting that she has ruined beef for me." He ruffled his sister's hair. "Fine. Eat whatever you need to, kiddo. I support you."

River wandered off, still holding Finn.

Sloane put her hands in her front pockets and eyed Rick.

He really was a good guy and she felt warm inside just watching him with his sister. "I'm serious, Rick. What you're doing with River is impressive. Not everyone could or would raise their sibling."

He shrugged, clearly embarrassed by the compliment. "It was me or foster care and there was no way. Not happening. But it's hard. I'm not going to lie." Then he eyed her over his raised beer bottle, hovering near his lips. "I'd rather impress you in other ways."

Of course he had to lighten the subject. She would do the same thing so it wasn't like she didn't get it. "Oh, you did. Trust me."

"Can I impress you again tomorrow night?"

The idea of repeating the night before instantly made her wet, nipples beading. She took a deep breath through her nose. She could not be turned on at her father's cookout. It was ridiculous. But Rick was giving her that look... the one that said he wanted to tease and touch her until she screamed in pleasure.

But at the same time, they had said one night. That's what she remembered. So what game was he playing? "I don't know..."

"Hey, Dick. I mean, Rick," Sullivan called. "Get over here. I need a corn hole partner."

She could see her brother impatiently waiting, Axl and Brandon down there as well. She didn't see Jesse but he might already be heading back to Houston, where he lived and played hockey.

"This isn't over," Rick said under his breath as he turned and yelled that he didn't want to be partners with a loser.

Sloane needed a cold drink. "Do either of you need anything?" she asked her girlfriends. They were lounging in lawn chairs positioned next to a spinach and artichoke dip platter. Lilly was over by the firepit chatting with her father and her aunt, her dad's sister.

"No, I'm good," Becca said.

"Same," Emily agreed. "And don't think you're going to get out of talking about a certain someone and a certain something. We want the scoop." She grinned.

Sloane was surprised they had waited this long to ask frankly. But she wished they hadn't asked at all. She didn't want to lie. But she wasn't sure she wanted to tell them about sex with Rick. It seemed so... private.

"I have no idea what you're talking about."

They gave peals of laughter. "Uh-huh."

Sloane opened the slider and went into the kitchen. The style and décor in the house were stuck solidly back in the early nineties. Her dad had never changed anything as far as she could tell. There was still a wallpaper border in the kitchen featuring cherry pies coolly on a fence post. Which seemed wildly impractical to her. The countertops were a forest green laminate. As a teenager, it had just embarrassed her. Now it made her worry about her father. He was holding on to the past with two fists.

He was chopping up onions on the peninsula. "Hey, baby girl," he said, glancing up and giving her a smile.

"Hey, Dad. Who's manning the grill?" She went straight to the fridge for a can of soda.

"Burgers and hot dogs are done. We can eat in a few minutes. And then, birthday cake for the birthday girl."

They weren't the family to exchange presents and she was fine with that. But cake, she could get behind. "Yum." She shut the fridge door and popped open the can in her hand. "So what's new, Dad?"

He gave her a skeptical look. "Nothing, Sloane. Not since I saw you yesterday."

"No, I mean, what is going on in your life." She leaned over the counter on the opposite side from him, watching his skilled knife work. He'd started out in the kitchen of a local seafood restaurant at sixteen. "Are you online dating or anything?"

Now he looked at her like she had lost her mind. "Where the hell did that come from?"

Resting her chin on her palm she shrugged. "Just seems like maybe you should. You're still young, you're handsome."

"Do you need to borrow money?"

"What? No!" This family. Geez. "I'm just showing interest and expressing concern."

His hand paused. Then he just started chopping again. "Did you hear from your mother or something?"

That shocked her into standing straight up. "Why would I hear from Mom?"

"I don't know. It was your thirtieth birthday. Just thought maybe she would reach out."

"No, she didn't." Sloane realized with a sinking feeling that her father still wasn't over it. Over her. She who will not be named. "Dad, it doesn't bother me. Seriously. I don't even care. What bothers me is you not leading a full life. I want you to be happy."

He shot her a look of horror. "I am happy."

"Don't you ever want to get married again?"

"Do you?"

"I don't know." Yes. If there was a man out there she could laugh with, share a dog with, have amazing sex with. Who would love her, flaws and all.

"Me either." He handed her a tray filled with burger toppings. "Take this out to the table."

"Sure. Good talk, Dad."

He shook his head like he didn't even know what they were talking about. "Yep."

"Think about Tinder, Dad. You'd be a hit. You can write 'hot grandfather, bar owner, loves tats, whiskey, and blondes.'"

"Shut up, Sloane," he said mildly, popping a spicy pickle in his mouth. "Or I will shut you up."

She laughed. "Love you."

"Love you, too."

That was about as emotional as an O'Toole chat was going to go. She'd take it.

SULLIVAN THREW a corn hole bag at him. Hard. It hit Rick in the chest before he could catch it. "What the fuck was that for?"

"For sniffing around my sister like a dog after a bitch in heat."

Shit. He'd been too obvious. "I don't think you should refer to your sister as a bitch in heat. Just saying," he said, keeping his voice neutral.

"You may be bigger than me now, but I can still kick your ass." Sullivan looked furious.

"You're going to start a fight in front of your kid and my little sister? Calm down." He turned and called over to Axl and Brandon. "Who's throwing first?"

"We are. Switch sides."

Rick took the bags and started to walk down to the other board but Sullivan grabbed his shoulder.

"Rick, listen to me."

His friend's voice was earnest, not angry. He paused and looked back at him. "Yeah?"

"I found out Tom was cheating on Sloane. She didn't say anything to us about it, so obviously she's having such a hard time. I don't want you fucking with her head, okay?"

He nodded. He had no intention of fucking with Sloane's

head. He would never do that to her. And he was honored she had trusted him both with her body and the information that her ex had cheated on her. "Sure. And maybe you should talk to each other more, you know? Like share feelings and shit. It might make all of you feel a whole hell of a lot better."

Sullivan made a face. "Fuck that. We don't do feelings."

"So I've noticed."

Brandon came over to their side. "What's the hold up, losers? Are we playing corn hole or grabbing our dicks?"

"O'Toole is dick-grabbing. Watch your junk." Rick jogged over to the other side.

Axl eyed him. "Sul knows you have the hots for Sloane, doesn't he?"

"Yep."

"Dude, you can't fuck your best friend's sister. Not good game play."

Rick tossed the bags in his hand up and down, in a lame attempt at juggling. One dropped to the grass. He bent over and accidentally made contact with Axl when he stood up.

"Shit," was Axl's opinion. "You already did, didn't you?"

"I'm not saying a word." He turned and tossed his first bag at the opposite board. It slid straight off.

"You deserve it if he kicks your ass. I might even have a go at you myself." Axl tossed a bag. It landed on the board.

"Don't worry about it, man. It's all good. I would never hurt Sloane."

Axl shook his head. "I don't like this. It won't end well. You know that."

"I've known Sloane my whole life. I'm not going to be an asshole."

"Don't tell me anything. I don't want to have to lie for you."

"I'm not asking you to lie. And I'm not admitting a damn thing." Rick threw another bag and it slid in right next to Axl's.

Sullivan threw and knocked Rick's bag off into the grass.

"We're on the same team," Rick yelled over to him dryly.

"I don't care."

"Yeah, he's pissed," Axl said.

"He can't prove anything." And never would if he and Sloane were discreet. He really didn't want to damage his friendship. "He'll get over it." Because he didn't think he could give up Sloane. Not yet anyway.

"Time to eat," Liam called.

Good. Maybe with food in his mouth Sullivan couldn't say something stupid.

All the guys, River, and Liam's own sister, Bridget, were all moving around the peninsula in the kitchen filling up plates. He reached for a paper plate and Sullivan shoved him out of the way. "Excuse me."

Sloane was holding Finn and she shot her brother a look. "Watch where you're going, Sullivan."

"Why, am I hurting your boyfriend?"

The casual chatter came to halt in the group. "What did you say?" Liam asked, glancing back and forth between Sullivan and Sloane. "Sloane, what's your brother talking about?"

"My brother is being an idiot," Sloane seethed. "Who doesn't know anything about what he's talking about."

Lilly tried to do her magic trick, where she touched Sullivan's arm and about fifty percent of the time he calmed down. It didn't seem to work this time though. Sullivan was fuming.

Liam turned to Rick. "Are you and Sloane dating?"

Oh, shit. He did not want to be put on the spot like this by a man he respected. He cleared his throat and told the closest approximation to the truth. "No, sir." Technically they were not dating.

"That's true," River said.

He could have kissed his sister for backing him up. He was going to buy her ice cream for the rest of the week.

"I mean, he has a lot of girlfriends but Sloane isn't one of them."

And... she blew it. "River," he said, giving her a warning look.

Emily laughed, biting a carrot loudly in the awkward silence.

"What?" River asked, pulling a super innocent face.

He wasn't buying it. She could manipulate circles around everyone in the room. She was just stirring the pot for excitement.

"Does someone want to explain to me what is going on?" Liam asked, scooping baked beans onto his plate. "Sullivan?"

"My best friend is trying to get with my sister."

At least Sullivan thought he was still in the trying phase. "That is not true." Because it wasn't. He'd already got with her.

"And that's your business, why?" Liam asked calmly. "Sloane is a grown woman."

"Sloane is straight off a divorce."

"And my wife left and your wife passed and neither of us want anyone to have any sort of opinion on us or what we do now. Extend the same courtesy to your sister."

Sullivan threw his still-empty plate down and stomped off. He went down into the basement, slamming the door behind him.

"Should I go after him?" Sloane asked her father.

"Nah. Let him work it out. He'll come around."

"Give me that baby," Bridget said to Sloane, reaching for Finn. "Go talk to your brother. None of you do enough talking."

"Don't do it," Liam said.

This was getting awkward. "Grab a burger, River. Let's go back outside."

"I'm a vegetarian, remember?"

"Right. Grab your fruit and let's go outside."

River was studiously sorting through the fruit tray. She seemed to have an aversion to melons, which took up fifty percent of the tray. Rick sighed.

This was the downside of having impulsively—after fifteen years of wishing for it—having sex with Sloane. The O'Tooles were his second family and now he'd changed the dynamic. There was tension in the air.

His fault. He hadn't been discreet enough when he was talking to Sloane. He'd touched her neck. And he'd talked to her too long.

He should fucking know better. He was used to being discreet. With River, it was essential. Sure, his kid sister was smart enough to put together two and two when it came to his dating, but she never saw anything first hand. He did all his dating when she was with their father or Rachel. He should have used the same rules when it came to Sloane. No leaning in to whisper in her ear. No singling her out.

So for the rest of the cookout he studiously ignored Sloane.

Even when Bridget lit candles on a cake for her, he hung back, trying to emulate what would be his normal behavior.

It didn't matter that when she bent over to blow out her candles he could see down her shirt, just a teasing glimpse at the pale flesh he'd in his mouth the night before. It didn't matter that he was picturing her lips wrapped around his cock, something he hadn't had the pleasure of enjoying yet.

He just shifted behind the breakfast table so no one could see the growing hard-on in his jeans.

Sloane tried to blow out all thirty candles in one fell swoop and failed miserably. A solid third of them were still burning and there were groans of disappointment. Her father said, "Geez, kid, you need to work out more."

"Yeah," River said. "You're really bad at blowing."

Fuck. The kid had no idea what she was saying, obviously, but he was already fixated on a blow job and this wasn't helping. He wanted to laugh, desperately. Rick tried to look anywhere but at anyone.

He almost succeeded to holding it together.

Then Sloane said, "Maybe I need to practice."

Maybe she didn't mean it dirty. But he fully aware of his thoughts taking a nose dive straight into the gutter. Without intending to, he lifted his eyes and met the amused gaze of Sloane.

He felt the power paradigm shift ever so slightly in her favor. She had him by the balls, wanting more, and she knew it.

Oh, hell, no. He wasn't giving up control that easily. He'd pined for Sloane all through school and then the night before the ball had been solely in his court.

He was going to wrestle it back.

Not now, with her family and friends standing around all watching them intently. But back at his apartment building, where the other two neighbors were a ninety-year-old woman, Mrs. Williams, who was hard of hearing, and a guy in his fifties who worked nights at the convenience store and slept all day long.

"Well, isn't this just so sweet?" Sloane's aunt Bridget said, looking intentionally clueless.

No. Sweet was Sloane's lips. Sweet was Sloane's pussy, hot and wet beneath his tongue.

Rick went and grabbed a beer. He was suddenly very thirsty.

NINE

SLOANE WAS LYING in bed Monday night, exhausted and wishing whoever was banging around in the shop downstairs would die a painful, torturous death. She had put in another full day at the groomers and then had come home, eaten a store-bought salad, and attempted to create some sort order to the chaos that was her apartment. She had reached the horrible point where you still have a dozen boxes but no damn clue where to put any of the items in them.

Really, why did she have an egg cooker? Her new kitchen was about five by five, with exactly four cabinets to store everything. The counter space was exactly three feet. She knew, because she'd measured it. Her kitchen in her house with Tom had been enormous, with professional grade appliances. Not that she was a gourmand by any means but she had liked to cook. The irony of that being Tom was almost never home; he was either at the hospital or getting called back to the hospital. She'd made herself some very delicious meals in a beautiful, big, lonely as hell house.

But here, she was struggling to figure out what to do with all her equipment and had come to the sad conclusion she was going to have to either ditch about half of it or take it to her dad's house. Which wasn't a horrible idea, either. She could cook for him once a week. The man lived on beer nuts, which could not be healthy.

As her thoughts spun around and around, she listened to the sound of an air compressor going off downstairs. Really? Her own thoughts were clanging and loud enough, she did not need Rick's night owl work habits preventing her getting a decent night's sleep. It was his fault all the way around she was sleep deprived, now that she thought about it. Saturday, he'd kept her up half the night—which was worth it—but then Sunday night she'd been exhausted and unable to sleep because she was worried about her brother. Sullivan had clearly sensed the sexual tension between her and Rick.

Now he was fixing something at midnight? Who did that?

Sloane closed her eyes and counted to ten, breathing deeply in and out. Draw the air in through her nose, push it out her mouth. She relaxed her shoulders, one at a time. Wiggled her fingers. Forced herself to relax the muscles in her thighs, her calves. Let her feet droop. The temperature in the apartment was perfect. She had the window cracked for a cool breeze and her sheets were crisp and new.

She started to drop into sleep.

Wham. The compressor went off again, jolting her out of her zen state as she jerked up off the mattress. Her heart rate increased twenty-fold. "That's it." She threw the sheet off of her legs and sat up. She was groggy and dizzy from the tease of repeatedly almost reaching REM and then being yanked back into reality.

Sloane stood up and stumbled across her bedroom. She'd decreased the number of moving boxes in there only marginally, not having enough time to deal with any of it, and she stubbed her toe on a heavy box corner. "Ow. Damn it."

Grabbing her keys off the kitchen counter so she didn't get locked out of the exterior door to the building, she left the apartment in sleep shorts and a tank top, shoving her hair out of her eyes. She wanted to murder Rick.

He may be sexy and he may have given her the best sex of her life but she needed some motherfucking sleep or there would be hell to pay.

She came tumbling out onto the sidewalk, not even caring if anyone saw her. But of course, no one did, because everyone else in Beaver Bend was, you know, *asleep*. Except for her landlord. The air was cool and downtown was quiet in either direction. Most of the buildings were shops, not residential, and it struck her now as a little eerie. Fear started to creep in to mingle with her anger.

The front door to the auto shop was locked but she hot-footed it around the side and found the garage door wide open. Rick was whistling along to the radio, which was turned to a low volume. He had a car up and was clearly working on it.

"What are you doing?" she asked. Which was a pointless question. She could see what he was doing. He was working. At midnight. On a Monday.

His whistling cut out and he turned. "Hey, Sloane. I'm working. What are you doing?"

"I'm not sleeping, that's what I'm doing." She moved into the garage, feeling like hissing as the bright lights hit her in the face. "You're really loud, are you aware of that?"

"My radio is on low." He gave her a smile. "You look very cute right now, did you know that?"

He put down whatever tool he was holding and came toward her. Sloane paused. Oh, hell, no. She knew that look. He was stalking her. He wanted her. Nope. Not happening. "You can't distract me, Rick. I'm exhausted and I'm pissed off. You either need to be quieter or quit working for the night."

"Sorry, beautiful." He came up to her and brushed her hair back off of her face. "I got behind on my regular repairs because I've been busy working on my bike you wrecked."

Oh, he was good. "That's not going to work, Ryder. I refuse to feel guilty because you are stubborn. It was an accident."

He kissed the corner of her mouth. "Hey."

She shivered, crossing her arms over her chest. "Hey, what?"

"We're alone and no one can see us in the back of the garage." He put his hand to her lips. "Unless you don't think you can be quiet."

His other hand was teasing at the front of her sleep shorts, right between her legs.

And just like that, she proved herself just as stubborn as him, because she was not about to let him think she couldn't control her volume.

She reached out and grabbed his cock through his jeans. "I'm not the noisy one. I think we just established you are."

RICK SUCKED IN A BREATH. Damn, Sloane had turned the tables on him. Completely.

She had stormed in there, looking sleepy and sexy, her hair a mess and her nipples jutting into the cotton of her tank top.

He did feel bad he'd woken her up. That didn't mean he wasn't going to take advantage of it though. So while she stroked his cock, he stroked her pussy through the thin fabric of her shorts. He dipped his finger deep, right between her lips. She sucked in a breath.

"Come here," he said. "Come see my handiwork. Truthfully, I owe you a thank you. The bike needed some TLC anyway."

He dropped his hand and reached for hers. She sucked in a disappointed breath. He grinned, wanting to draw out the anticipation. Sloane in his garage at midnight, ready and willing? Dream come true. He wanted to see her straddle his bike. Arch her back. Show him those nipples.

"You're welcome," she said, dryly.

That made him laugh. "I feel like you're being sarcastic with me."

"Then you feel right."

"At least your insurance premium won't go up. You should be grateful to me."

Her eyes darkened. "Oh, I am."

Fuck. He tugged her hand and drew her to the back of his garage, where his bike was parked, ready to ride again. Shiny and polished, his pride and joy. "There she is. Better than brand new."

"Looks nice."

"Nice? All you can say is nice?" He was only half-kidding. "This is not a nice bike. It's bad-ass. It's a bobber-style Indian."

"I have no idea what that means but if it makes you happy." Sloane yawned.

That was not acceptable. "Here, climb on." He held his hand out. "It's thunder black smoke, with a custom trim color. I had this thing built exactly the way I wanted it. I've had a thing for motorcycles since I was a kid."

Just like he had with Sloane. Now as he helped her climb on, he figured this was as good as it was going to get. Sloane on his bike in a tight tank top. She looked hot as hell. She had long lean legs, spread wide to accommodate the bike.

Glancing at him, clearly amused, she tossed her hair, raking it off her face. It did fantastic things to her chest. Rick reached out and cupped her tit, giving it a gentle squeeze. "Don't you feel bad ass?" he asked. "Because you look bad ass."

"I feel a little bad ass," she admitted. She grabbed the handlebars. "Are you going to take me for a ride?"

Rick adjusted his cock in his jeans. "On the Indian? Another day. But I can give you a different kind of ride."

She laughed softly. "Four on the flirt scale. Too predictable."

He thumbed her nipple, which had gotten nice and firm for him. She wanted him as much as he wanted her. "Oh, and you're unpredictable?"

She nodded. "I can be. I used to be all the time. Then I seem to have forgotten now. But now that I'm back in Beaver Bend, I'm remembering how carefree I used to be."

He liked where this was going. "That's a good thing then."

She sat up again and peeled off her tank top, exposing those delicious tits for his full view. Rick swore under his breath. She tucked the tank top into the waistband of her pink sleep shorts and rose up a little, clenching her thighs. Hands in her hair, she gave him a sassy look. "Do I look like a pin up girl?"

He nodded, slowly, backing up so he could really appreciate the view. "I'd buy this calendar that's for damn sure." He pulled out his phone.

"You are not going to take a picture of me." But she didn't change positions or look alarmed in any way.

"I am if you say it's okay." His dick was so hard it was throbbing painfully in his jeans. His tongue felt too thick for his mouth.

"I should be worried about an evidence trail." She bit her lip, which only made him groan again.

"And?"

She threw her leg back over the bike, disappointing him even more than he had been when the Vikings lost in the play-offs. But then, magic happened. Sloane didn't dismount the bike. She just eased her sleep shorts down, giving him a flash of her dark curls before kicking the shorts onto the floor.

"What are you doing?" he asked, fucking scandalized and as turned on as maybe he'd ever been.

"This." She lifted her leg again and the view he got nearly killed him.

"Fuck," he said, already reaching for her.

But she waved him away and settled down onto his bike. She shivered. "Oh, that feels kind of dirty."

"It's a lot dirty. And gorgeous." He had to shift his feet apart to give his dick more room.

"No, I mean it's cold steel on my warm body."

He could see goosebumps were marching across her arms. "Your body or your pussy?"

She bit her lip. "Pussy."

He'd never be able to ride the Indian again without thinking of Sloane straddling her, bare ass and pussy resting on the machine. She had no idea what she was doing to him. None. Or maybe she did and she liked torturing him. But he didn't think so. She was just exploring, having fun.

"I should keep you awake more often."

That made her laugh. "Please, I beg you, no."

"You're begging me?" Rick put his phone back in his pocket. "I like the sound of that."

She rolled her eyes. "Where is River, by the way?"

He did not want to think about his sister. "Tucked in bed, asleep. I have the building under surveillance and she's all locked in. Both to the building and the apartment. Please don't call me a bad parent. I get that enough from my father. He thinks she'd be better off living in his mold-infested hellhole than with me."

"I wasn't going to judge you, trust me. I think given you're right downstairs, it's totally normal. How it is any different from parents hanging out in their suburban garage when their kids are inside sleeping?"

That made him feel better. She had a point but he'd been feeling too guilty to even consider that. "Thanks, Sloane. Now can we talk about the fact that you are completely naked on my motorcycle and there is no one to hear us or interrupt us?"

The tip of her tongue crept out of her mouth and slid along her bottom lip, moistening it. She made a show of spreading her legs even further, and leaning forward. It was an absolutely fucking fantastic view. The curve of her ass rose, beckoning him to grab on and squeeze. Her tits jutted forward, and her neck was long and graceful. The perfect silhouette. She was a motorcycle magazine cover.

"We can talk about it," she said. "Or we can just do something about it."

"Ride or die?" he asked, as he pulled his wallet out of his jeans and grabbed a condom. Then he ditched his T-shirt and his jeans and approached the bike.

Sloane gave him a sly smile. "Definitely ride or die."

Rick cupped her cheeks and gave her a hot, bent up kiss, letting all his passion loose on her. She destroyed him she was so damn sexy. When he pulled back she was panting. "Stand up, beautiful. I'm sliding in."

She did stand up but then she said, "Now what?"

Leaving his briefs on because he was not about to stick his bare ass on cold steel he took her around the waist and hauled her to him. "Wrap your legs around me."

She did, her tits pressing against his bare chest. Her arms snaked around his neck.

It was an intriguing tangle of limbs but he managed to get up on the bike, with her facing him, and eased her down into his lap. "Hello," he said. "Funny meeting you here."

Sloane gave a seductive little laugh. She didn't giggle, that wasn't ever her style. She had a husky voice, one that could hold him as securely as a fist wrapped around his balls. "I know, right?" she asked, arms draped loosely over his shoulders.

The skin on her thighs had cooled from sitting on the bike,

goosebumps still prominent all over her body. He aimed to make her warm again. Starting with bending down and easing his tongue over her nipple. She arched her head back to give him better access and he drew the tight bud into his mouth. He scraped his teeth over it and she gasped.

His cock was resting on her thigh, still covered by his briefs. Ripping the condom open with his teeth, he set her back slightly, lifted his cock out and sheathed it. Sloane was already rocking against him eagerly and he teased her apart with his fingers, testing to see if she was ready for him. He cursed. "Babe, you're so wet."

"It's the motorcycle. I got turned on."

"And here I thought it was my muscles."

Sloane gripped his shoulders. "Fuck me, Rick. Just shut up and fuck me."

He didn't need to be told twice. He gripped her waist and eased her down onto him. She gave the most seductive groan that he lost all ability to hold back. He just palmed her hips and pounded up into Sloane.

Gravity kept her firmly on his cock and she was moaning virtually nonstop, her tits bouncing up and down with the hard rhythm. The bike was hard beneath him, the artificial lighting of his garage cast down over Sloane at an angle. Her body was fully displayed and lit for him, yet her face was in shadow. Her voice told him all he needed to know though. Her head was thrown back and she was holding on to hard. He was going to have bruises on his shoulders tomorrow and that turned him on even move.

Her clit was rubbing against him from the angle and she was getting frantic, her moans desperate. He eased a finger between their bodies and tweaked her clit, giving it a little pinch like he'd done her nipple. Her head gave forward and she locked eyes with him, her mouth open in shock.

She came silently, a big beautiful orgasm, so intense he felt her pussy contracting on his cock. He could feel her slickness sliding down over him.

Finally she dragged in a deep breath and gave a soft laugh. "This is so dirty."

"Yes, it is." He drove into her, wanting her to understand how hard she made him. "You like my ride?"

She nodded. "Best I've ever had."

That stroked his ego just enough to cause him to explode. He was fucking Sloane on his Indian and she loved it. He buried himself inside her and let go of the last shreds of his control.

Sloane watched him, looking triumphant as he groaned out her name. She even laughed softly, looking every inch the confident girl he'd known in high school.

If he could help her heal from her marriage in any way, he was happy to do it. Especially if it involved sex. It was his special talent. Not to brag or anything. Okay. He was bragging.

"But you never saw this one coming back when we were kids." He exhaled on a sigh. "Damn, that was hot."

"Nope. If anyone had told me I'd be having sex with Little Dickie, naked on his motorcycle, I would have thought they were a few fries short of a Happy Meal."

"Unexpected. It keeps life exciting."

Sloane shifted a little. "Help me down off this thing. I'm not as limber as I used to be."

"You seem pretty flexible to me, though I may have to test it further. Splits, remember?" He winked at her.

Sloane rolled her eyes, like he knew she would. He stood up and lifted her down off the bike. When she bent over to get her shorts and tank top, he swatted her bare ass.

"Ah!" she shrieked, jerking away. She covered her ass and shot him a glare. "You're a very bad boy."

He grinned. "The worst. But you're a very naughty girl. Who stripped herself naked on my bike."

She tilted her head. "That was pretty naughty, wasn't it?"

"Yep."

"Good," she said, looking very sassy. She pulled her tank top on. "Now please tell me you're done working so I can get some sleep."

He wasn't where he had wanted to be but he'd lost his enthusiasm for carburetors. He wanted to walk Sloane to her apartment and give her a goodnight kiss.

"I'm done." He adjusted himself and retrieved his own clothes. He took a deep breath. "Ah. Sex and motor oil. My two favorite scents."

"Gross!" Sloane laughed and put those little shorts back on.

"It's not gross. It's the smell of awesome." He wished he could slide into her bed and hold her throughout the night, but he wasn't comfortable leaving River all night, even if he was just across the hall. She knew he worked at night, but if she woke up at five in the morning and he wasn't there, she would get scared.

"All right, I'm heading up."

"I'll walk up with you."

"Won't that look obvious if someone sees us leaving together at midnight?"

Rick raised an eyebrow as he felt his pocket for his wallet. "Sloane. If they see you leave here at all they might speculate. You're in your pajamas and there's no fire."

"I'll just tell them the truth—I came down to yell at you to keep it down."

He had no idea who these mysterious people were who were going to question her on her nocturnal activities but he just nodded. "Solid plan."

It turned out the mysterious people was a nine-year-old girl.

When they came up the stairs River opened the door and poked her head out. "Why are you guys together so late?"

Busted. "What did I tell you about opening that door?" he demanded of his sister, annoyed because one: she'd almost given him a heart attack. And two: now he couldn't kiss Sloane goodnight. "You know you're not supposed to do that."

River rolled her eyes. "I heard your voice."

"I went downstairs to yell at him," Sloane said. "I was trying to sleep and he was banging around down there. It was totally rude."

"Totally," he said, amused. Zero hesitation on her part to throw him under the bus. "Sorry again."

"It's okay. Partly my fault anyway since I hit your bike Saturday night."

She sounded more snarky than sincere but he wasn't going to worry about it. "Goodnight then, Sloane. See you around."

River held the door open wide for him. "No one likes a workaholic."

He grabbed her around the neck and gave her a noogie while she squirmed. "Who body swapped you with a fifty-year-old woman? Your soul is so old it makes dirt look young."

"Weird." River shook her head. "You're just weird." Then she pulled away from him and waved to Sloane. "Goodnight."

Sloane was unlocking her door and she turned back and smiled and waved at him.

She looked sleepy and sexy, her hair wrecked, her lips pink and plump. Her neck was still stained red from sexual exertion. She looked like everything he'd ever wanted.

Rick felt something he'd never experienced before.

A niggle of doubt that he could stay casual.

He hustled River into the apartment and slammed the door, fucking terrified of that thought.

TEN

SEE YOU AROUND.

The words stuck in Sloane's craw for days.

That had been Rick's goodnight to her? See you around.

See you the fuck around.

She sprayed a beagle down with warm water, massing shampoo into his haunches. The dogs were the only thing keeping her sane because she wanted to go shove "see you around" up Rick's tight ass.

She had stripped naked and posed on his motorcycle and he was going to see her around? He'd seen every damn inch of her. Fucking Little Dickie.

She shifted the sprayer too far and water bounced off of Harley's shoulder and ricocheted into her eye. "Damn!" She swiped at her eye. "At least I got myself instead of you, buddy." She bent down and massaged his ears, giving him a kiss on the top of his head. He watched her with trusting brown eyes. "You are very, very cute."

The bell rung over the front door and she glanced over, realizing she'd been hoping it was Rick. It wasn't. It had been three days, including her Wednesday day off, and she had not seen him. It was River coming through the door. Sloane wondered why River spent her days in and out of the garage and the groomers. Didn't she have any friends? Wasn't there a camp she could go to? Day care? It seemed boring to her. But then again, River was always reading or watching a movie on an iPad. She didn't seem very outdoorsy or athletic.

As kids she and Sullivan had been outside all summer long, riding bikes and roller blading and playing hockey. She hadn't sat down to watch TV at all. There had been tumbling classes and cheer camp and bonfires with her friends over.

"Hi, River, what's up?"

"Interest rates." She shook her iPad. "And the DOW is down."

Nope. River was not at all like Sloane had been as a child. Not even close. She admired Rick even more for raising her because Sloane honestly wouldn't have a clue what to do with her. "Interesting. I hope you don't lose your shirt in the stock market."

"Nope. Sold at the right time." River reached out and rubbed Harley's head.

"Are you being serious. You own stock?" Sloane finished rinsing Harley and moved the dryer over him.

"Yep. Not a lot, but Rick usually gives me fifty bucks on my birthday and I invest it."

"Good for you. But dang, I'm clearly failing at adulthood."

"Are you divorced?" River asked.

"Yes."

She nodded. Didn't say anything, just nodded. Like she agreed Sloane was failing at life.

Great. A nine-year-old thought she was a loser. "So what brings you by?"

"My brother wants to know if you and Winnie want to go to

lunch. He said he is dying for a burger. I refuse to participate in murder so he needs someone to go with."

So Rick wanted to go to lunch with her and Winnie. She was not feeling it. But there was no way to say no if Winnie wanted to go. Her boss heard from the other wash station and said, "Burgers? I'm in. I'm so in."

"You can go then and I can stay here."

"No, we can both go."

"Who is going to stay with River and the dogs?" she asked Winnie. "No, you go. I'll stay. I'm not even hungry."

She wasn't. What she wanted apparently wasn't on the menu.

River eyed her, like she understood something was off about Sloane's reaction. "Don't feel bad," she said. "He keeps girls he likes in the Friend Zone."

She wasn't sure how she felt about River. The kid was on the edge of unnerving. "What are you talking about?"

"If he likes you as a person, he Friend Zones you. Girls he doesn't care about are the ones he dates."

"I have no idea what you're even talking about," she said flatly, tempted to stick her head under the dryer with Harley.

"I think you do." The miniature sage gave a knowing nod.

"I really don't. I don't think I'm as smart as you, River." What she thought River was saying was that Rick liked her as a person so he wasn't going to have sex with her. Which meant, since he had had sex with her, that he did not see her as a friend. But another notch on his bedpost. That wasn't surprising, but that didn't mean she had to like it.

In fact, it made her really damn cranky.

She could admit, having Little Dickie crush on her had been ego-boosting.

Have adult Rick attracted to her was equally satisfying.

But if she was just the flavor of the week she wasn't sure how she felt about that.

Which was one hundred percent insane because she had assured him that all she wanted was a fling. That it wouldn't be weird or awkward.

And now she was hurt because he hadn't reached out to her in three days.

Stupid.

She was just stupid.

"Oh, here's my brother." River put her finger to her lips. "Shh."

Rick strolled in through the front door, hands in his front pockets. It was really unfair how good-looking he was. His presence filled the waiting room. It wasn't just his big body. It was his confidence and cocky swagger. That charming grin.

Sloane studiously ignored him, checking Harley's coat, then drying her hands on a towel.

"Hey, ladies," he said, moving past the desk into the salon. "Ready for lunch?"

"Hi," Sloane said, determined to sound normal. "I'm going to stay here with River and the dogs. Winnie will go with you."

He just nodded easily. "Okay, then."

He didn't look disappointed.

And she was disappointed that he wasn't disappointed.

Oh, my God, she'd become that girl.

The one who swore she could have a hookup then get pissed off when that's all it was.

Her phone rang in her pocket while Rick was strolling around petting the three dogs they currently had in the salon. She pulled it out to see who was calling and was surprised to see it was her former neighbor, Maribeth. She had been a bright spot in her life in Minneapolis. A dozen years older than Sloane, she had always been up for a glass of wine and some gossip. She was probably just calling to see how Sloane was doing.

"Hello?"

"Sweetie, I'm so glad you answered." Maribeth sounded agitated.

"Is everything okay?" Sloane asked. "How's Patrick?"

Patrick was Maribeth's husband. "Oh, that asshole is fine. He's golfing today, thank God. Listen, I'm calling because I'm really upset and I don't know how to tell you this."

Her gut clenched. "Tell me what?" Was Tom living with Javier? Had they gotten married in Vegas? If it was that, she honestly didn't care. There was no point in holding on to bitterness over her ex's infidelity.

"It's Kate."

Sloane's knees buckled. "What about her?" She couldn't handle it if something had happened to Kate. Tears welled up in her eyes even before she knew what was wrong.

"That dick you were married to has her chained up in the yard. She's been there day and night for over a week. I went over the first few days and made sure she had food and water and played with her, but now Tom has locked the gate and I can't get in. Her water dish was empty both days I got in there."

Sloane was horrified. "What?" Kate was her baby. The thought of her suffering in any way made her knees buckle. She wanted nothing more than to hop in her car and drive to Tom's and hug Kate close to her and reassure her. "Oh, my God, why the hell would he do that? It's probably eighty degrees outside in Minneapolis!" She started pacing back and forth, unsure what to do.

"Should I call the APL? I can't even get water to her now with the gate locked."

"If you call the APL will they put her down?" Sloane couldn't handle the thought of that. "I should be able to contact my attorney and have an investigation opened, right? I mean, he won Kate in the divorce but this is neglect and abuse."

"In theory, yes. But how long will that take? I'm going to call Tom and try to reason with him. Me calling is different than you calling him."

"Thank you," she said, voice trembling. "And thank you for letting me know." The words got caught in her throat. "If something happens to her, I don't know what I'll do."

"Let's touch base later today or tomorrow. Don't worry, sweetie, I'll knock the fence down with my bare hands before I let anything happen to your baby."

"Thanks, Maribeth. I can't thank you enough."

She ended the call and realized Rick was watching her, concerned.

"What's going on?" he asked.

Sloane burst into tears.

"Hey, hey, it's okay." Rick reached out and pulled her into his arms.

She let him, though she didn't wrap her arms around him. She just held her hands in an x over her chest, mind racing. "It's my dog. That was my old neighbor. She said my ex has had my dog outside for over a week solid, and doesn't appear to be feeding her or giving her water on a regular basis. It's hot outside right now and there isn't much shade to speak of. And the bastard has her chained up, which is not something I ever did. The yard is fenced! Why chain her up?"

That miserable fucker. That absolutely horrible son of a bitch. He hadn't wanted the dog. He had just wanted to hurt her, which made no sense. She had been a decent wife to him. She hadn't bitched about his hours as a doctor. She hadn't overspent his money. She hadn't cheated. What the hell had she ever done to him that she deserved this? Yes, she'd blown up at him when she'd found out he was cheating, which seemed to astonish him. She wasn't known for sharing her feelings and it seemed like Tom had thought she'd just quietly accept it. Which she had, after one explosion. She'd told him the one good thing she'd gotten out of their marriage was Kate.

Somehow Kate had wound up the pawn because of those words, which made her feel sick and sorry she'd spoken up at all, even in impulsive anger.

Poor Kate. She was a helpless victim and Tom was a stranger to her. She didn't know this side of him. But then again, maybe his sexuality wasn't the only side of himself he had been hiding from her.

Rick rubbed her back. "That is a real dick move. Is the neighbor going to call somebody?"

She shook her head. "No. I'm afraid they'll take her and put her down. She's seven. I'm going to call my lawyer and see if there's anything I can do to get her back, and Maribeth said she's going to go over and talk to Tom and see if he'll be reasonable."

"That all sounds like a good plan." He pulled back and wiped the tears rolling down her cheeks. "Let me know if there's anything I can do."

Sloane sniffed, trying to get her emotions in check. She had to call her lawyer. "Thanks, Rick. I appreciate it." She turned to her boss, stepping away from Rick. "Winnie, is it okay if I call my lawyer? I can still watch the salon while you're at lunch."

"Oh, my gosh, sweetie, of course. Rick and I can take a raincheck on lunch anyway. Rick?"

"Agreed. I just had something come up anyway." He had pulled his phone out of his pocket and seemed to be texting someone.

"Okay, thanks so much. I'll go in the break room." She rushed to the back and called her lawyer but he was at lunch. She left a message and came back out, chewing on her fingernail as she fretted.

Rick and River were gone.

Winnie gave her a look of concern. "What did the lawyer say?"

"Nothing. I had to leave a message."

"Do you want to take the rest of the day off?"

Sloane was super grateful she worked with someone who loved animals as much as she did. "Thanks so much, Winnie, but honestly, I'd rather stay busy."

"Whatever you need. I have tequila in the back room too if that helps." Winnie gave her a wink.

Sloane laughed nervously. "Give me an hour and I might take you up on that."

RICK WALKED BACK into the garage and told his intern, Blake, he was taking the rest of the day off. "You can handle being here alone, right?"

Blake was twenty, a bright kid with an eye for detail. He was also fast. He could break down and rebuild a cylinder in record time. Rick felt confident leaving him alone for a few hours.

"Sure, no problem. Everything okay?"

"Yep, just need to take care of something." He couldn't stand to see Sloane cry. And he couldn't stand to see bullies get their way. It was a hot button for him.

River gave him a long look. "You're going to go get that dog, aren't you?"

The kid was scary perceptive. There wasn't even any point in denying it. "Yes."

"That's illegal, you know." River leaned on the countertop where his computer was and rested her head in the palm of her hand. "I can't bail you out if you get arrested."

"No one is getting arrested." He ruffled her hair, wondering when the age would arrive where she would care enough to brush it. "Besides, you have plenty of cash. You probably could bail me out."

"Haha." She chewed her lip. "I just don't want anything to happen to you, okay?" She looked like she might cry.

Rick was touched. "Nothing is going to happen to me. I'm just going to make sure that gate gets opened and if the dog happens to walk out and down the street and jump in my car, then that's not a crime. I am just picking up a stray."

"She said the dog is chained up." River stood up. "You haven't even thought this through!"

"Right." Details. He wasn't so much into them as River was. "I'll figure it out." One thing he had learned in life was if you just brazened and shouldered your way through life, it usually worked out.

"Can I go with you?"

"No."

"I'm a good cover. No one will think you're breaking and entering with a kid with you."

She was good. He was constantly amazed at what a little manipulator River was. Some day she was going to destroy a lineup of men. They would topple like bowling pins under her machinations.

"We should take your bike," he said. "You can't ride it so we'll look like a father teaching his daughter to ride a bike."

"I like it." She stuck her hand up and out for a high-five. "I'll put on my T-shirt with the dog on the front. For good luck."

Rick slapped her small hand with a high five. "Let's do this." This was most likely the world's worst parenting ever but wasn't he teaching her compassion? "You do understand I'm doing this because I'm afraid if we wait for the bureaucrats to do their thing, Sloane's dog could die from dehydration, right? I don't normally advocate just driving around setting dogs free."

"I get it. Besides, you like Sloane."

"Of course I like Sloane. She's Sullivan's sister. We grew up together."

"Whatever." River rolled her eyes. "Because you want to be a hero to just a random girl you grew up with?"

Rick couldn't help but laugh. "River Anne Ryder. You are one in a million. Love you, kid."

"I love you, too. Now get your tools."

"Yes, ma'am." He saluted her and went to grab a bolt cutter.

Then he called Liam and explained what was going on. "I just need the address and I don't want to ask either Sullivan or Sloane." Sullivan would have an attitude and Sloane would fret about him.

"I should tell you this is a dumb ass idea and not to go."

"But?" Rick would do it no matter what but he'd prefer not to have Liam pissed at him.

"But I'm not going to do that. Sloane loves that dog and you know I love dogs. Anyone who would do that to an animal is an asshole and I've half a mind to go with you."

Rick grinned. "You are more than welcome."

"The problem is Tom knows what I look like, obviously. I'm going to have to sit this one out."

"Good point."

"I'll send you a picture of the dog. She's a beautiful Golden Retriever."

"Awesome, thanks."

River came back into the shop as he was ending the call. She had a bag packed. "What's in there?" he asked.

"Snacks. For us and for the dog."

"Cool. We need to stop and buy a dog leash."

Twenty minutes later they were on the road and Rick felt a rush of adrenaline. He wasn't going to question too closely why he was driving three hours to steal a dog for Sloane. He was going to insist to himself it was because they were friends and first and foremost he couldn't stand the idea of a dog suffering.

But it was also because he couldn't stand to see Sloane so upset.

It had skewered him.

He cranked up classic rock on the radio as he drove, despite River wrinkling her nose at it. He had started to take his truck but then realized he might have better luck getting the dog in his Mustang. Nice and low to the street. It might not entirely fit into the neighborhood. He had the impression it was kind of a ritzy house, but rich people had hobbies too. Surely someone with money liked a good classic muscle car.

River was right. She was an excellent cover.

The kid might be a genius but she had the eye-hand coordination of a newborn.

He wasn't even sure what the hell she was doing wrong, but she could not stay on that bike to save her life. "Lean forward," he said, as he walked along beside her. They were approaching the house Sloane had lived in with her ex.

"You just told me to lean back!"

"You overcompensated. Find neutral."

"What does that mean?" She straightened herself on the seat, the handlebar twisted and she would have fallen if she hadn't put her foot on the ground.

The bike had been a birthday present from him the year before and honestly, biggest waste of sixty bucks ever. River had briefly admired the shiny pink seat and ran her fingers over the glittery handlebars. He had spent a hellish few hours trying to teach her how to ride it before she had declared it stupid and pointless and that was that.

"It means neutral," he said. "Where your body is naturally at ease."

"My body is at ease on the couch," she said, biting her lip in concentration.

Rick laughed. "Don't be a wimp. It's for the dog, remember?"

"I know. I'll stick it out, but don't you think I should be wearing a helmet?"

She might have a point but he wasn't about to admit that. "How are you ever going to be going fast enough that you'll need a helmet? Relax."

Rick discreetly checked out the neighborhood. It was a quiet street. Given it was a Thursday at three in the afternoon he had to assume most of the residents were at work. But there were no kids playing outside at all. Which meant no witnesses. Yet at the same time he and River did stand out like a sore thumb. If anyone asked he would have to give a vague story about living on the next block.

It didn't seem like they were going to see a soul though. The houses were big and stately, built in the last decade or so. It didn't make Rick jealous of Sloane's ex. He didn't give a damn about money other than that he wanted it to be comfortable. He had a pretty hefty bank account in his own right and he didn't aspire to a big house. Too easy to accumulate stuff. And he wasn't big on stuff.

When he was a kid, he had imagined growing up and living in a mansion but never all that seriously. Mostly, he'd just wanted a house that wasn't littered in animal hair, molding food, and piles and piles of newspapers. Sloane's house was a red brick colonial, like the other houses on the street. He supposed he could picture her living there. Yet at the same time he struggled to envision her as a housewife, filling her days with volunteering and cleaning the house. It must have been a lonely marriage, for damn sure.

River righted her bike and attempted to pedal yet again. "I

think I should start walking it," she said. "We're never going to get there."

He'd parked his car down the block, right around the corner out of view. Their plan was a little shaky to say the least, but he didn't think it was going to be a big deal because there was no one around. He could easily say the dog was loose and who could question it?

Which was what he told himself as he hauled his six foot four frame over a fucking wooden fence that could have protected the damn Alamo. Who the fuck needed a fence this high when they lived in the suburbs with neighbors two house lengths away and a shit ton of trees? The guy probably never even used the backyard. Rick decided he hated Tom as he ripped his favorite jeans on the drop down.

He was wearing a ball cap low over his face on the off chance their was surveillance cameras. Liam had said there wasn't but you never knew. The guy might have gotten paranoid in the last few months.

The second he turned he spotted the dog. She was hugging the house, curled in a ball, trying to keep her body in the shade. She was panting and looked exhausted and miserable. "Fucking unbelievable." Rick wanted to find Tom and chain him up. Leave his ass in the yard.

"Hi Kate," he said, approaching her cautiously, down low, hand out.

She waved her tail and stood up. The chain made a clanking sound that grated on his nerves. He petted her behind the ears and looked around. The yard was overgrown and neglected. There were flower pots on a stone patio but the flowers were dead. He spotted the hose laying carelessly in a bed of bushes and he went over and turned it on. He was planning to cup his hands and fill them but Kate started drinking straight from the stream of water.

"Poor little girl, thirsty, huh?" He let her go for thirty seconds or so then turned it back off. He removed the collar around her neck that held her to the chain. She shook her head, clearly delighted.

Yellow fur flew up in his face. Rick laughed. "Better, huh?"

She came in and licked his face.

"Now we just need to go out the gate and we're good."

Kate readily followed him to the gate by the side of the house and wagged her tail. He was torn between looping the leash around her neck or not. It would make any sort of story about finding her loose look like bullshit but he decided he didn't care. He'd rather she were safe, in his grip, and in his car without incident.

So he put the leash around her neck and tied it up.

The gate was locked on the inside so he just undid the lock and opened it.

Only to find a woman standing on the other side swinging a baseball bat at him. "What the hell?" he asked, dodging her wild swing.

"What are you doing with that dog?" she demanded.

"I know the owner. Who are you?" he asked.

"Hah. Nice try. I live next door and I saw you climb over the fence like a no-good dog thief."

Praying this was the same neighbor who had called Sloane he said, "Maribeth? I'm Sloane's friend. I came to rescue Kate."

She eased up on the baseball bat. "You know Sloane?"

"Yes. I was there when you called her today."

Maribeth had wild curly hair and a sassy stance. "I'm going to need to verify your story."

"Sure. No problem." Rick kept a firm grip on Kate and his distance from Maribeth's bat. He couldn't see River and that was starting to concern him. River didn't like him doing anything risky. Hell, she didn't even like him going fishing because she was convinced he was going to drown or catch a flesh-eating disease. She was forever afraid a car would crush him. He did not need her to see a suburban vigilante swinging a bat at him.

Nor did he want to be forced to restrain Maribeth.

"Sloane? Listen there is a guy here springing Kate. He says he was with you when you got the call from me earlier. He's very tall, has a five o'clock shadow, and biceps that make me wish I was single."

"I can hear you," he told her. Though he did appreciate the compliment.

She waved him off and told him, "I need to see some ID."

Really? He pulled out his wallet and flashed her his driver's license.

"That picture doesn't do you justice," she said. "You're much better looking in person."

"Thanks." He gave her a slow, sensual smile that might move this process along a little faster. "So I'm free to go?"

"Yes. Sloane says you're on the up and up."

"Good, because standing on Tom's property probably isn't the smartest thing I've ever done, and my little sister is up on the sidewalk and I need to get back to her."

"That little girl trying to ride her bike belongs to you? Saddest thing I've ever seen. She has zero coordination."

Rick led Kate out of the backyard and past Maribeth, who only moved slightly. "It's okay. Her intelligence makes up for her lack of agility."

"Sloane wants to talk to you." She held the phone out to him.

"Hey, beautiful, what's up?"

"Are you nuts?" she screamed in his ear. "You drove to Minneapolis to steal my dog? Are you insane?"

"Something like that."

She exhaled in his ear. "Is she okay?"

"She's fine. Just exhausted and hot and a little scared."

"Thank you," she said, her voice breaking. "You don't know what this means to me."

His chest felt tight. "You're welcome."

"Are you sure she's okay? You wouldn't lie to me, would you?"

"She's fine, I swear. I wouldn't lie to you about that."

"Oh, my God, this is such a relief."

"I'll have her back to you in a couple of hours."

"Thanks, again, seriously. I owe you something extra special," she said, her voice growing husky. "Anything you want. And I mean that."

If she was offering sex, he was taking it. He'd spent three days tortured by the memory of Sloane on his bike and he felt like he'd slipped backward in time. He was jerking himself off in the shower to thoughts of her. She was still the hottest girl in Beaver Bend.

But he'd started to freak himself out that he was feeling too much.

This was different though, right? If she wanted to show her special appreciation who was he to say no?

"We can discuss that when I get back. I just have one question—do you still have your cheerleading uniform?"

If he was getting offered fantasy sex on a platter he was going with his oldest fantasy. Sloane in her tight cheerleading top and short-ass skirt.

She gasped. "Oh, you are a dirty son of a bitch, Rick. I like it."

He cleared his throat. "I'm handing the phone back now before we get in real trouble." Trouble that had nothing to do with trespassing and everything to do with phone sex with a witness.

She laughed softly. "Kiss Kate for me and I'll see you soon. Thanks, Rick. You are the best."

That made him ridiculously proud. He expanded like a puffer fish.

But while he was busy patting himself on the back Maribeth was swearing under her breath. "Take the leash off of Kate and let her loose. The asshole is home!"

"Oh, shit." Rick slipped the leash off of Kate and took off running, assuming she would follow him.

She did. Like it was a game. He cut up through what he hoped was Maribeth's yard and took off for River, who was walking her bike and looking scared. The dog was keeping pace with him.

He could hear Maribeth talking to presumably Tom, who then called for the dog. "Kate!"

Rick tried to make it look like he was trying to capture Kate. He wasn't sure how successful he was being. Then River screamed, like she was afraid of dogs, and dropped her bike. She cut across the street, cutting right through the yard that led to his car. Kate, clearly gleeful to be free, ran straight after her.

Damn. Kid was brilliant as usual.

Rick grabbed her bike and followed.

When he burst out on the next street, River was sitting in his car with Kate, her snack bag open.

He threw the bike in the trunk and jumped in. He started the engine and got the hell out of there. "We're out of here."

"Thanks. Want a pretzel?" River asked.

"You talking to me or the dog?"

"Either of you."

"I'm good." He glanced over at her as they left the housing development. "We did it. If you ever tell Dad about this I will deny it, just so you know."

River scoffed as she fed a pretzel to a very eager Kate. "I can keep a secret. Like, for example, I know you are goo-goo-gah-gah for Sloane and I haven't said a single word about it."

"Goo-goo-gah-gah? What the hell is that?" He was keeping an eye on his rearview mirror to make sure they weren't being chased. "Isn't that what babies do?"

"Well, maybe. But I mean you look at her and you're all 'ooh, Sloane, beautiful.' You're squishy and weird."

"I'm squishy and weird? We're friends, River. That's all."

"You're in love with her." She popped a pretzel in her mouth and spoke around it, pretzel bits flying out of her mouth. "I know des tings."

"Don't talk with food in your mouth," he said automatically.

River may be smart but what the hell did she know about adult love? Nothing. Her mother had followed the example of Rachel's mother and his mother and rolled on out on her kid. There were no examples of healthy marriages in River's life, so he was going to assume for whatever reason she had it in her head that this could be a thing.

She was wrong.

Because sure, he liked Sloane. He'd been lusting after her for years. He thought she was smart and compassionate and generous. That wasn't love.

Or was it?

Fuck.

"Give me a pretzel."

ELEVEN

SLOANE TOOK Winnie up on her offer and cut out of work early. She drove over to her dad's house. "Hey, Dad, are you leaving for Tap That?" she said, calling him from the driveway.

"Five minutes. What's up? Are you in the driveway? Come in."

"Yeah, okay. I just wanted to go through my old room and some of my stuff." To look for her uniform. She thought it was likely it was still there because her father didn't throw anything away.

"Sure. Stay as long as you want."

She got out of the car as her father opened the front door. "You hear anything about Kate?" he asked. "I heard there was an issue."

The pieces clicked into place. She went up the walk. "So Rick called you, huh? He's the only one who knew about it, and clearly someone gave him Tom's address."

"Guilty. And I regret nothing. I'm guessing your dog is fine since you're smiling?"

"She is almost here. Rick said they're about thirty minutes

out. She's fine, she was just thirsty and hungry, and probably bored."

"Good. That's great news." He let her into the house and followed her. "He's a good kid."

"Who, Rick?" she asked, amused to think of Rick as a kid. In a mere week her opinion of him had totally changed. Gone was her brother's annoying friend. Now he could only think of him as a fully grown man.

"Yes, Rick. He must like you to do something like that."

Shit. Here it was. "Dad. Please stop. He doesn't like me. We're just friends-ish." He felt bad for her, that was all. He liked her body, sure, and her company with no strings-attached. But he didn't like her, like her.

"Whatever you say, sweetheart. I'm off to the bar. Lock up when you leave."

"Will do." Sloane ran up the stairs and opened the door to her bedroom. It was like an homage to the mid-2000s. Complete with *Mean Girls* quotes on the wall and posters of O-Town, her boy band crush at the time.

Everything was exactly the way it had been the day she left for college. The closet was empty of clothes but her dresser wasn't. It had all her old school spirit T-shirts and some random pajamas and funky socks. Then there it was—not her official cheerleading uniform, because the school had owned that. But the less expensive one they had used for parades and pep rallies and had to pay for themselves. She distinctly recalled her father bitching about the cost of it, making her wash glasses at the bar as her contribution.

She took it downstairs and found a plastic grocery bag where her dad had kept them for the last twenty years. Left hand side of the pantry, stuffed in a brown bag hanging from a plastic hook. Shoving the uniform in, she wondered if there was any possible way she would still fit in the damn thing and left, locking the front door.

Her weight hadn't really fluctuated much but she definitely had more booty than she had back then. She'd been known on the squad as "Flat Ass." That, coupled with somewhere in the neighborhood of an extra ten pounds and Rick was in for the legitimate slutty cheerleader experience.

When she got back to the apartment building, she got a text from Rick.

In my apartment.

She ran up the stairs, shoving the plastic bag in her purse so River didn't get too curious about it. Impatient to see Kate, She knocked on the door to Rick's apartment. When it opened, Kate came flying out at her. "Oh, my goodness, hi, baby." Instantly she started crying. Kate looked thin and her coat was dull. "Hi, hi."

Going down on her haunches, she laughed when Kate jumped on her and knocked her back on her ass. "That's my girl." Hugging Kate to her she looked up at Rick. "You're amazing."

"No big deal. Glad to help." He actually looked sheepish.

Sloane closed her eyes and just held Kate, overwhelmed. She felt so horrible for having let Kate down. "Has she eaten?"

"Yes, I got some dog food on the way home."

"I'm going to take her downstairs and give her a luxury spa experience. She smells like dirt." She kissed Kate's head and stood up. River was hovering the doorway. "River, do you want to help me?"

"I would but my dad is coming to pick me up. We're going to dinner and a movie."

"Oh, okay, that sounds fun." She smiled at her. Her heart rate kicked up a notch. That meant she and Rick had a few hours. Alone.

"I'll help you," Rick said.

"Perfect."

They heard a knocking on the door downstairs to the apartments. River ran into the apartment and hit the buzzer to unlock it. "Dad's here," she said.

Sloane was curious to see Rick's father. She didn't remember ever really meeting him as a kid. Rick had said he was a hoarder which meant he clearly had a clinical disorder or some sort of mental health issues. But like she imagined a lot of hoarders were, nothing about his appearance gave away his living conditions. He was cheerful, smiling as he came up the steps. He was a slightly shorter, thinner version of Rick. Older than her own father, he was attractive. Clean, tidy clothes and a clean shave.

"Hi, son, how's it going?"

"Good, Dad. How are you?"

"Can't complain, can't complain." He stuck his hand out to Sloane. "Hello, young lady, I'm Ralph."

"Nice to see you." She shook his hand. "I'm Sloane O'Toole, Sullivan's sister."

"Is that right? Wow, look at you. All grown up." His eyes swept over her appreciatively. "Did you move back home?"

"Yes, I've been back a few weeks."

"Well, if you're looking for company, I'm available."

"Dad," Rick said, practically snarling. "She's thirty years younger than you."

He shrugged, giving an "aw, shucks" smile that somehow managed to not be creepy. "So is River's mother. Love is love, Rick." He pulled River into him to give her a hug. He kissed the top of her head. "What's up, Girl Genius?"

"Just genius works. No need for a gender qualifier."

"Got it. But anyway, the invitation is there, Sloane."

"Don't mind my father," Rick said. "He doesn't understand subtlety."

"You're as big of a flirt as I am," Ralph protested.

"He's right," River said.

Was that Rick's future, to morph into his father? Sloane wondered if he ever thought about that.

"Thanks," she told Ralph. "But I'm straight off a divorce. I'm focusing on me for right now."

And Rick.

There were goodbyes and promises to have River home by ten, then she and Rick were alone in the hallway. "Come in for a second," he said. "I need to put on shoes."

Rubbing Kate's head and telling her, "Come on, girl," she followed Rick inside. She'd been so focused on Kate she hadn't noticed he was barefoot. He definitely made the whole T-shirt, jeans, no shoes thing super sexy.

"I'm sorry about my father. He doesn't seem to grasp he's in his sixties."

"It's fine. And hey, like he said, River's mother went for it, so who am I to judge?"

"River's mother has borderline personality disorder. She's very extreme. She was all in for about four months, obsessed with my dad, then she was out. My father seems to have an uncanny ability to pick out women who are as compulsive as he is. Like my mother. Rachel's mother."

"That's really sad," she said, and she meant it from a place of compassion. "It must be hard to always be chasing that intensity."

"I'm sure it is." He watched her glance around his apartment. He was very neat. The place was spotless. Maybe even stark. Probably a reaction to the way he'd grown up. "Do you talk to your mother?" she asked. "I barely remember mine." She watched Kate wandering around the apartment, sniffing here and there.

"Nope. Last I heard she was in Mexico working at a resort as a singer." He sat down and reached for his shoes. "It's kind of weird, isn't it? We both grew up without our mothers."

She sat down beside him and touched his knee, briefly. "I say it doesn't matter to me, but of course it does. You know none of us O'Tooles talk about our feelings. I'm sure that's the reason. Plus I think I married Tom because he had a career and I thought I could have everything, you know? The marriage, the house, the kids, the dog. It's all I've ever wanted." It made her feel wistful. "I don't understand how my mother could walk away from all of that."

"I guess because she wasn't you," he said simply. "But yeah, I totally understand where you're coming from. I always loved being at your house because to me, you had a normal family. I know my father's actions affect me. No doubt about it. I don't want to be that guy," Rick said, shoving his foot in his sneaker. "The one who tosses the word love around like it's no big deal. Who makes promises of a fucking castle in the sky and how he'll treat her like a princess and none of it is true. It's a run-down house filled with garbage. Literal garbage."

Sloane wanted to touch him, but wasn't sure she had the right. "I'm sorry. For what it's worth, I think you're amazing for being a surrogate father to River. She's going to grow up knowing she was loved by both you and her father."

"That's the other thing," he said, turning to look at her earnestly. "What woman is going to want to be a part of my life? I live in an apartment with my kid sister."

Sloane thought there were plenty of women who would easily take on that role. "It's no different than being a single dad. It doesn't drain your entire dating pool."

Kate seemed to realize Rick needed a hug. She nudged

between his legs and licked his hand. "Get a dog? Is that what you're telling me?" He rubbed her head.

Sloane didn't know what to say. What she wanted to say was that there were women who would be thrilled to have a man in their life who took care of the people he loved. Who ran a business and still managed to laugh. Women like her. But she didn't want to make it awkward between them so she just said, "I think you can have whatever you want."

He gave her a small smile. "That's always been your motto, hasn't it?"

She wasn't sure that was a compliment or an insult. "I guess so."

What she wanted was him.

And she was starting to think for more than just sex.

For real and for forever. Because she and Rick were two sides of the same coin. He grew up insecure about his looks and his living conditions, while she hadn't. But then the end of her marriage had brought out all those feelings of unworthiness in her, so they understood each other. And yet, despite some bumps along the way, and neither having a mother, they both were people who just wanted companionship. A family. Easy happiness.

The way she felt when she was with him.

Sloane jumped up, terrified by her thoughts.

She didn't want to ruin their friendship.

Or his friendship with her brother.

And she didn't want to lose what they had by pushing for more.

"Let's go give this stinky girl a bath," she said.

"HERE, let me help you rinse her," Rick said, taking the sprayer. He hit Sloane in the chest with a stream of water. "Oops."

She jumped back and gasped. "Oh, you are so going to get it for that."

Rick laughed. "How? I have the sprayer."

She made a grab for it, but he pulled his arm back. "I'm taller and stronger than you. You'll never get it back." Even though he was a little preoccupied by her now-damp shirt. It was clinging to those delicious tits. Unfortunately, her shirt was dark gray so the view wasn't as good as it could be, but the fabric was making her nipples obvious.

"No?" she asked. Her hand slipped over the front of his jeans and she found his cock easily.

She stroked him up and down.

"Damn, Sloane. Straight for the kill."

"Give me the sprayer."

"No. I promise to behave." Rick made a concerted effort to turn and rinse off Kate, who was standing in the dog wash like she had found her bliss. She was calm and seemed to enjoy the water.

Sloane gave him one last stroke and let go. "Fine. I'm holding you to that."

"Keep an eye on the time," he said. "I don't think Dad will bring River home early but we better stay aware. And we probably should go to your place if that's okay."

"For what?" she asked, feigning innocence. "I don't recall having plans with you."

"Cute." He used his free hand to reach behind her and squeeze her firm ass. "You told me anything I wanted I could have. I want this tight little ass."

"You mean, actual anal?" she asked, eyes widening.

Rick's dick got hard. "Well, no, I meant your ass figuratively. I didn't know that would be on the table. Is it?" That was exciting. He got a lot of push back on up the ass because his cock was too big for most women to handle comfortably.

"I don't know. I mean, maybe. I guess we'll see." She looked intrigued.

Rick groaned. "Beautiful, you're killing me. What happened to the woman who told me her sex life was vanilla?"

"You," she said. "That's what happened."

Holy shit, that was hot. "Kate, you're looking great. I need to take your mommy upstairs now and fuck her brains out."

Sloane covered Kate's ears. "Not in front of my child." She toweled Kate off.

"Is the dog going to be okay?" Rick asked Sloane after Kate hopped down, all squeaky clean and grinning in happiness. "She isn't going to weird about us getting it on, is she?"

"I don't think so. But I don't really know. She's never watched me enjoying sex before."

Rick laughed before he realized that wasn't really funny. "Sorry. Too soon?"

She shook her head. "It's fine. It's funny now because I never even really knew my sex life sucked. But I don't know about role playing as a cheerleader. That's a lot of jumping around."

Jumping around sounded like something he wanted to see. "Maybe we should put her in my apartment for an hour. We don't want to stress her out."

"True. Isn't she a sweetheart?"

He nodded. "She's a cool chick just like you." Kate was a very calm dog, especially considering everything that had happened to her the past few days. Hell, the last three months. He was pretty sure that's when Sloane had gotten divorced.

She put a leash on Kate and they went back upstairs. The dog didn't even protest when they put her in Rick's apartment. He conceded to give her a pillow and a blanket and let her sleep on the couch. He closed the door to River's room. There was a stuffed animal village in there that might be tantalizing to Kate.

"Sit down," Sloane said, when they were in her apartment. "Make yourself comfortable. I'll be a minute."

She had done more unpacking. There were only a few boxes sitting around still. She had hung up some personal photos. One of Kate. Two of Finn. One of her, Sullivan, Liam, and Kendra at Sullivan and Kendra's wedding. The smile on Sullivan's smile made him sad for his buddy. The guy had loved his wife so much.

What would it be like to love someone like that?

Sloane walked into the living room and every thought Rick had left his mind. He was pretty sure his jaw hit the floor. "Holy shit..."

She posed in the doorframe, raising her arms up, which lifted the tight sleeveless top even more. She grinned. "What do you think? It still fits, but barely."

In the dozen years since high school Sloane had developed more womanly curves so that her old uniform was clinging to her tits. The skirt had raised on her waist, pushed up by her more generous, making it short as sin. He had a view of legs that went on forever, long and lean. One false move and he was going to see her panties. He couldn't wait.

"It fits like a glove."

She laughed. "Hardly. But given the look on your face, I'm going to assume you approve of the tighter version."

"Oh, I do, baby, I absolutely do." He wanted to touch her, run his hands up under that skirt but he didn't want to cut short whatever she was planning. "Give me a B."

There was a B for Beaver Bend emblazoned on the shirt. The uniform was a royal blue with gold lettering. Their mascot had been a hawk, which made no sense for a school called Beaver Bend High. He and his friends had all been disappointed they couldn't make beaver jokes at school events.

"I'm kind of sad I don't have pom-poms. That really would have sealed the deal."

"I don't even miss them," he said in total honesty. "I don't want any of you covered up."

She walked into the living room and spun, so that her skirt twirled from the sharp movement. He almost caught a glimpse up her skirt but not quite. Back to him, she touched the screen on her phone. *Jock Jams* came blaring out.

"Oh, yeah," he said. That song took him right back to high school and pep rallies and lusting after Sloane. "Bring it."

On the beat, she whirled back around and bent over, swinging her head so that her hair went flying. She remembered the dance routine. She actually fucking remembered it and she was hitting every move. Every rock and arm motion, a sultry expression on her face. He sat there and got hard as fuck watching her. What made him actually swear out loud though was when she did a kick and he saw right up under that tiny skirt.

No panties.

He saw everything she had for one brief amazing moment before her leg came back down. She moved closer to him with some kind of cheerleader voodoo that had her moving her arms and legs in a way that propelled her forward. He didn't know what any of it was called, just that it was destroying his ability to form words.

When the music came to an end, and she turned and stomped off, shooting him an arrogant look over her shoulder, he clapped. It was a performance worthy of applause. "Babe, you killed it. That was fucking hot."

She turned and dropped the smoldering expression. She started laughing, a little breathless. "That was fun, I admit it. Maybe I should start going to dance classes as a hobby."

"I'll pay for them," he said. "Especially if they're pole dancing classes."

Pulling a face, she came over and stood over him, placing both palms on his chest. "You're very bad."

"Says the girl not wearing panties." He put his hands under her skirt, cupping her tight little ass. "See? Bare as the day you were born." He squeezed that tender flesh and she gave a soft cry of surprise and pleasure. "Stand up, Sloane. I need my pants off yesterday."

She stood back up and gave him a pout. It wasn't a very Sloane expression and he drew her back to him and kissed her, sinking his teeth into her bottom lip. She gasped.

"No pouting," he murmured against her mouth. "I'm going to make you very happy in about sixty seconds."

"Promise?"

"Promise."

She stood up and put her hands on her hips. "I'm not sure I can get this top off all that easily. I may need your help."

Rick shook his head. "Oh, the top is staying on. That's part of the fun."

Sloane laughed. "I can't believe I'm doing this. We're ridiculous."

"No. We're awesome." Instantly that sounded a little too much like they were a couple, but Rick covered it by peeling his T-shirt off. That way he didn't have to make eye contact. He didn't want to come across as wanting more from Sloane than she could give.

Dropping his shirt, he tugged her hand. "Over here." He pulled her to the end of her couch. "Turn around." He pushed on her back, so that she bent over. Her ass rose enticingly in that tiny skirt. The bottom of her cheeks peeked out from under the fabric.

She splayed her palms on the arm of the couch and glanced back at him. "Oh, I see where this is going."

"Yep. And I'm going to pull your hair too, while I'm fucking you." Rick reached under her skirt and eased a finger between her thighs and drove it deep into her pussy. "Look what I found."

"What?" she breathed, arching her back and shifting her legs open even further.

"A wet, sweet pussy."

"Imagine that."

He eased in and out of her, moistening up her clit with her own slickness, listening to her breathing change, grow deeper, more frantic. When she came it seemed to shock her. She moaned.

"What the hell?" she asked. "I didn't mean to do that."

He drew his hand down over all that thick hair and gave a soft laugh. "The point is to do that."

"But not so soon."

"I'll give you another one. Don't worry."

First, though, he was going to prep her for something he wanted to try later. Not today, but he had to start somewhere. And he refused to think about the fact that he was assuming there would be a "later."

Nope.

Not going there in his head.

So instead he took his slicked-up index finger and he teased it into Sloane's ass.

She jerked but then gave a small cry. "Oh, my. Oh, wait... oh, Rick, that's not bad at all."

"Good. This is just a little practice for another day. We'll get there in stages. Because now that it's in my head, I can't let it go."

"It's very different but interesting." She was gripping the couch tightly.

Rick pulled her skirt up so he could have a full view of her sweet ass. "Are you ready for my cock in your pussy?"

She nodded. "Yes. So ready."

Rick shoved his jeans down and took one for the team.

TWELVE

SLOANE HAD NEVER FELT sexier in her entire life.

Which was insane. She was in a cheerleading uniform.

As Rick kicked her legs further apart and slid inside her, she groaned. "Oh, damn, that feels good."

Being with Rick felt freeing. Like she could just totally let go and have fun. Noting was awkward or off-limits. He'd found her dance hot instead of ridiculous and she had felt good doing it. Thirty and she still remembered that routine.

His rhythm started out slow, then he really went at her hard. She was shocked by how fantastic that felt. Her entire body tingled with sexual tension and she leaned further so that she wouldn't shift. The slap of him pushing inside her was better when she was immobile. She liked it hard and deep, who knew? Not her, that was for damn sure.

"Sloane."

"Yes?" Her eyes were half closed and she was starting to feel frantic. As desperate as the rhythm he was using to drive into her. Dancing for him had gotten her wound up, then the shocking feel of him teasing into her ass had driven her wild. There was just something about knowing he had yanked her into uncharted territory that was sensual beyond anything she'd ever experienced.

It made her wonder what heights of desire they could reach together.

If they were together.

"Scream my name. Let me hear how much you like being fucked."

She hesitated. She wanted to but she had never done that. Never let go that much and screamed out her pleasure. She didn't scream out about anything. She kept everything in, nice and tight.

Rick's callused fingers entwined in her hair and he yanked it back. "Oh, damn!" she said. Not because it hurt but because the sharp sting was unexpectedly arousing.

"Scream, baby. I want you to scream."

Sloane closed her eyes and blocked out everything but the way Rick was making her feel. The way he was taking her so hard, and filling her so completely. And as she tipped over into an orgasm, she finally fully let go. Her voice rose, like her orgasm, keening and urgent and excited as she screamed his name over and over.

"That's it, beautiful. So fucking perfect."

Rick yanked her hair again, bringing tears to her eyes, as he exploded with her.

It was vibrant and electric and it felt Rick had kicked down the boarded up walls around her and let her out. This was her. The real Sloane. The woman who liked sex and laughter and a dirty joke.

As they both found their release and Rick slowed to a stop, Sloane lowered her voice. Her throat was hoarse from yelling and she became aware that her hips were being crushed by the piping on the couch. But she was boneless and satisfied. Drawing in a shuddery breath, she said, "How was that? You finally nailed a cheerleader."

"It was like the Stanley Cup and the Super Bowl all wrapped up in one." Rick exhaled, and eased out of her. "I can't thank you enough."

That made her laugh. "The pleasure was all mine."

Rick helped her up and flipped her skirt back down. He was tipping his head to kiss her when they both heard it. The door downstairs open and River running up the stairs, chattering away.

"Shit," Rick muttered. "That's the end of my fun for tonight."

"I want to check on Kate," River said loudly.

Now it was Sloane's turn to swear. "Shit, she's going to knock on the door any second and I'm in a cheerleading uniform." She bolted to her bedroom, abandoning Rick to his own devices.

"Really?" he called after her.

Her response was to slam the door shut. She would die if River and Ralph saw her role playing with Rick. It would be mortifying. Absolutely mortifying. She pulled on panties under the skirt, then sweat pants. Unzipping the skirt and shoving it down over the sweats she heard Rick using the kitchen sink, then opening the front door.

"Hey, kiddo," he said, sounding like a birthday clown. Manic and creepy over-the-top cheerful.

"What are you doing at Sloane's?" River asked, sounding super suspicious.

Grappling with the top, Sloane tried to tug it off. "Damn, it's stuck." She was sweating bullets and smelled like sex and now she was stuck in this thing. Not trusting Rick to stay discreet she yanked again, arms over her head and crossed in an effort to try to pull it up. Nothing budged.

Giving up, she dragged out a sweatshirt. She yanked in on

over the top, her hair going in all directions. She was burning up, but it would do for now.

Rushing out into her living room she waved. "Hey, guys!" Great, now she sounded like she'd been sucking helium. "How was dinner?"

"Fine. Where's Kate?"

"She's in your apartment. Rick was helping me hang some pictures and I didn't want her to get scared. You know, all that drilling."

Rick's head whipped around and he coughed into his hand, amusement flashing in his eyes. "Lots of drilling."

"Oh. I'll go get her," River said.

Fortunately she didn't look like she thought that explanation was stupid, which it was. Rick's father was a different story.

"Too soon after your divorce, huh?" he said, grinning. He gave her a wink, which made him look a lot like Rick. "Sorry we're home so early. The kid was worried about the dog."

"It's fine," she said, adjusting her sweatshirt. The damn uniform top felt like she was wearing a seaweed wrap. Moist and tight.

"Not really," Rick said. "But five minutes sooner would have been much worse."

If she had been wearing a shoe she would have thrown it at him. He was all but admitting they'd had sex. It was probably pretty obvious but he didn't need to confirm it. But there was no time to chew him out because River came running in with Kate, who was leaping up and down excitedly.

"I'm so glad she's okay!" River said, sounding like she'd eaten a bowl of sugar for dinner. Or three cans of Mountain Dew. "Bye, Sloane!" She grabbed Rick by the arm. "Come on. I want to show you the new iPhone Dad got me."

Rick's smile fell off his face. "You bought her an iPhone?

You could have checked with me first, you know. She's nine and on electronics too much already."

"She's my daughter. I don't need your permission."

Uh-oh.

Rick said, "We'll talk about this later," in a tight voice. Then he turned and said, "Goodnight, Sloane. Talk to you soon."

"Goodnight," she said, weakly.

They all disappeared across the hall and she sank down onto her couch, dew on the back of her neck from overheating. That was a lackluster ending to a fantastic night. "Come here, Kate," she said. "I am so happy to see you and I really need your cuddles now."

Kate jumped up beside her and nuzzled her head under Sloane's hand. She called Maribeth. "Thanks for covering for Rick," she said after their hellos. "What did Tom do?"

"Tom concluded Rick was a Good Samaritan trying to help. He thinks she got out when the lawn maintenance crew showed up to spray."

"Oh, good. So is he looking for her?" She pulled Kate in closer, like Tom was going to appear out of nowhere and snag her.

"No. He actually said 'good riddance.' I wanted to punch him, but restrained myself since you have Kate safe and sound."

The idea of what might have happened to Kate made her sick. She hadn't thought Tom capable of such cruelty. If she had followed legal channels and waited for her attorney, what would the outcome have been? "Thanks, Maribeth."

"Okay, now let's talk about the hottie. Are you having sex with that man? Because if you are, I am so jealous of you. If you aren't, why the actual hell not?"

Sloane hesitated. But then she spilled, because she couldn't tell anyone in Beaver Bend. "Yes, I am, and holy moly, it's amazing."

"Well, duh. I mean, his muscles have muscles. Please tell me he's thrown you against a wall."

"No. But we had sex on his motorcycle."

Maribeth whimpered. "Stop. That is just... wow. So are you dating or doing the dirty?"

"Just doing the dirty." She sighed. "I've known him since high school. We kissed in a bathroom at a party once."

"Sloane, watch yourself. You're in a vulnerable state right now and the man drove several hours to rescue your dog. Be guarded."

That was the problem. She'd spent her whole life being guarded. "He's my brother's best friend," she said, which was not really a response. "We're sneaking around so Sullivan doesn't find out."

"Oh, sweetie," Maribeth said. "Too late. You're already falling for him. I can hear it in your voice."

She was but she resented that it was that obvious. "I just said it was a secret! How is that indicative of deep emotion?"

"If it was just a hookup you wouldn't care what your brother thinks. You've known in your heart since the beginning you might want more."

Her friend's voice was gentle and full of the wisdom of an older woman. Sloane realized not for the first time, this was what it might have been like growing up with a mother. "I don't see how that's possible," she murmured. "We called him Little Dickie in high school."

"Dickie or not, be honest with yourself."

"Yeah, sure. I'll call you tomorrow." Tonight she needed to put a cold compress on her aching head and reevaluate her entire life.

"Sure, sweetie. Take care."

Sloane ended the call and turned to her dog. "Kate, we have a problem."

Her dog gave a soft woof.

"I think I might be falling for Rick. It's either that or I'm so used to bad sex I've confused myself what the difference between love and lust is."

Kate barked.

"Yeah, that's what I think too. Any man who raises his sister and rescues a dog is worth falling in love with. I mean, I always like Rick, as a person. And seeing him now, the way he lives his life, I think..." That they were perfect for each other. She couldn't bring herself to say that out loud.

Because her brother would lose his shit.

And Rick was a perpetual bachelor.

And she had a history of attaching too soon.

"Oh, my God, I feel like I'm burning up from the inside out." She felt feverish and frantic as she yanked off her sweat-shirt. "I wish you had thumbs. I think I'm going to have to cut myself out of this top."

But at the same time she was reluctant to trash the top so after much twisting and turning and tugging she got it up to her neck. It was rolled like a burrito, but she was able to shove it completely off. She exhaled and breathed a sigh of relief as cool air washed over her hot skin.

She sat on her couch topless, petting her dog, and wondering what on earth she was supposed to do now.

RICK FOLLOWED his father and River into his apartment but then he told River immediately, "Go take a shower and get ready for bed." He wanted to talk to Ralph.

She made a face. "It's eight o'clock."

"You can read in bed."

River dragged her feet but she went into her room. He rubbed the back of his neck and tried to hold on to his patience.

"Dad, you can't just buy stuff for River without talking to me about it. Something like an iPhone means I have to monitor her activity on it, apps, social media. It's a whole can of worms that you just dumped in my lap."

His father shrugged. "What's the big deal? Every kid has a phone now. Didn't you want a phone when you were in high school?"

Rick wanted to point out high school and the fourth grade were two completely different things, but that would get him nowhere. "Can you just show me the respect to run it past me? My whole life you've never respected me."

"Oh, here we go. Now we're going to drag the past into this. You didn't have a bad life, so don't go acting all high and mighty."

His patience was quickly eroding. "We had to wash dishes in the bathroom because you had too much crap in the kitchen sink. We couldn't use the stove because you had boxes on it to the ceiling. My cat disappeared and we found his skeleton three years later under a mountain of old magazines that fell on him. My childhood wasn't stellar, and that is why River lives with me." It was just so frustrating to deal with his old man because he never took responsibility. "But that's not even the point. None of it is the damn point. The point is, I'm raising your daughter. I am. That's the reality and I'm happy to do it. I love that kid with all my heart. But don't make it harder for me by not respecting those boundaries."

It wasn't often he threw reality right at Ralph. His father sniffled, shifted his lips, crammed his hands in his pockets. Finally he said, "Yeah, all right. Whatever you say, kiddo."

Not exactly an admission of guilt or an apology but he'd take it. "Thanks."

"I'm heading out." His father headed for the door.

"Okay. I'll talk to you later." Rick looked across the hallway to Sloane's apartment door, willing it to open. He hated how they had been interrupted. He hadn't even gotten to give her a goodnight kiss.

What the hell were they doing? He'd talked about his mother with her. About his frustration with his father. She'd talked about her marriage. Not a lot, but he had a feeling they were both sharing more than they ever did with other people. This was no longer a teen fantasy for him. This was a friendship growing and developing and becoming something much, much more. Only he had no fucking clue how to handle that. Sure, Sloane was opening up to him. But he'd spent most of his adult life having women want him for the outside package, not nearly caring all that much who he was on the inside.

It was the irony of growing up and out of his Little Dickie persona. Sure, it was great to be considered attractive to women, but it had been a long time since anyone had attempted to get to know him. He didn't really know what any of it meant or what Sloane wanted.

River came out of the bathroom in a T-shirt and cotton shorts. It was clear to him she had gotten her hair wet without washing it. It was matted and flat and when she buzzed past him to the kitchen she did not smell like soap or shampoo. She smelled wet and dirty. What the hell was with the lack of hygiene at this age?

He followed her into the kitchen where she had opened the fridge. "Did you wash your hair?"

"Yep."

"Did you wash your body?"

"Yep."

"Did you brush your teeth?"

"Yep."

He waited until she stood back up. Then he held his fingers up one at a time. "Lie, lie, and lie. You smell like a worm farm.

Get back in there before I take you down to Paws and Effect and shampoo you myself like a mangy Labrador."

She looked unperturbed. "If I were a dog, I'd be a Jack Russell Terrier."

"Why is that?"

River tapped the side of her head. "Intelligent."

"That's true. But they're also highly trainable and you are not."

She made a face. "Do I really have to shower again?"

"Yes. Why do you want to walk around smelling like wet hair?" He found it hard to comprehend. At her age, he'd been painfully self-conscious and had worked hard to just blend in and be the funny guy.

She didn't answer him. Instead, she said, "You know, if you want to have a real girlfriend, instead of your girls who send you dumb pictures of themselves posing like this." She paused to stick her hand on her hip, drop her mouth open, and put another hand up in her wet hair. "You can, you know. I don't care."

He wasn't sure if he was amused or horrified. He did get a lot of pictures like that. Or ones where women were mostly naked, but looked surprised by the fact. Or the ones where they tugged down the neckline of their tight T-shirt, legs spread wide. He liked those pictures generally speaking, or he had until Sloane had come back to town. He just wasn't aware his sister had seen any of them. "What do you know about those girls?" he asked, reaching in the fridge for a beer. This conversation required an action for his suddenly nervous energy.

"I know that you don't care about them."

That didn't sound right. "They're friends, that's all. Girls I talk to, flirt with. But that doesn't mean I don't care about their feelings."

She rolled her eyes. "That's not what I mean. I mean, if you want like a real girlfriend, it's fine. Like Sloane or whoever."

There it was again. The little matchmaker. He wanted to grin but just took a sip of his beer and leaned against the countertop. "Do you think Sloane would want to be my girlfriend?"

River nodded. "Sure. Who wouldn't want to be your girlfriend? You're a nice person."

That touched him more than he wanted to admit. He suddenly had a lump in his throat. "Thanks, kid. I love you, you know that, right?"

"Of course I do. I love you, too." She chewed on the tip of her wet, unwashed hair. "So are you going to make Sloane your girlfriend?"

River seemed to want a commitment. "It's not that simple." It had been a long time since he'd had a real, honest to God girlfriend. "She might not want to. Or she might not want to upset her brother."

That made his sister scoff. "Why would he care? He's an *adult*. I'm a kid and I don't care, so why should he?"

She raised a valid question. "You know Miss Kendra died. That makes stuff complicated."

River looked unconcerned. "So are you going to ask Sloane?"

She was pushing, hard. He almost wondered if she had an agenda, but she looked sincere enough. "You don't think it's too soon?"

She shook her head. "Someone else might snap her up or she'll see those girls sending you those dumb pictures and then it's all over."

Fair enough. "Got it." He ran a hand over his sister's damp hair. Man, he loved this kid. She was something special. "Now wash your hair for real this time."

"Shampoo is bad for the environment."

There it was. "So look up online how to get clean hair without ruining the watershed. And while you're at it, look up summer camps for geniuses. I think you should go to camp next summer and meet kids who share your interests."

"Will I have to play sports?"

"No. Not if you don't want to. But you'll meet smart kids."

"Okay. I can go. But you owe me a favor then."

This kid. "I don't owe you squat."

"I want a dog."

Jesus. "We live in an apartment and there are a million dogs downstairs at Winnie's. Sloane has a dog. You don't need a dog right now."

"Maybe we should move into a house."

His heart squeezed. She wanted normal. River wanted a normal life. Just like he always had. Damn, he wanted to give that to her.

But all he said was, "You're pushing your luck. I'll think about a dog."

What could he say? He was a sucker for girls and animals.

THIRTEEN

SLOANE EYED Rick over the grill in the park three days later. "You don't know what you're doing, do you?"

They were across the street from their building, letting Kate romp around with River, while Rick was trying to con her into believing he knew how to use the park's charcoal grill.

"You light the charcoal on fire and let them burn. It's not that hard," he scoffed. "I know what I'm doing."

"Uh-huh." She had a sneaking suspicion this was the first time he had grilled a damn thing. But she wasn't going to push the issue. She was just happy he had invited her.

They weren't exactly being secretive. Winnie was joining them in a few minutes as soon as she finished up at the salon, and her boyfriend Todd was en route as well. They looked like friends who all shared the same address getting together on a beautiful summer day.

Nothing unusual about that.

Except that her feelings for Rick were complicated.

Seriously complicated.

He was gorgeous, no doubt about it. She felt the sizzle between them every time she glanced over at him. He made her body hum, and he always gazed at her with total intensity. When he winked at her, she wanted to tear his clothes off and climb on him. He was wearing a form-fitting green Packers T-shirt and shorts and he looked comfortable. He wasn't trying to be sexy, but there was no hiding those biceps and that broad chest. She wanted to grip his beard and kiss him, hard.

But their hookups were a secret and she was starting to hate that.

She didn't even know if he was still talking to other women, or meeting up with them.

The thought irritated her. It was his right to do that, but she still hated the idea.

"Why are you looking at me like that?" he asked, tearing open the charcoal bag and pouring the briquettes into the basin of the grill.

"Like what?"

"Like you want to both kiss me and slap me." His tone was mild-mannered, as it usually was.

He wasn't right though. Yes, she wanted to kiss him. But the only person she wanted to slap was herself. "I don't know what you're talking about."

"What, you don't like to kiss me?" he asked, shooting her a grin as he squirted lighter fluid onto the grill. "Here we go again. Destroying my ego all over again."

Sloane glanced over to make sure River was out of earshot. She was tossing a stick for Kate, who was enthusiastically bounding after it. Both the dog and the girl seemed to be bene-fiting from the new friendship. It thrilled Sloane.

River was too far away for her to overhear so Sloane turned back to Rick. "You want the truth?"

His eyebrows shot up. "I don't know, do I? That sounds ominous."

"Last chance," she told him, taking a step closer to him

around the grill. She was wearing a pair of tiny denim shorts and a cute top that showed off her breasts to fabulous advantage, if she did say so herself.

"Truth," he said. "Hit me with it."

She got as close to him as she could without it looking too inappropriate to any passerby or Winnie, if she popped up. "I did like that kiss in high school. I got wet from that kiss. I was grinding myself against your cock and I liked it."

His nostrils flared. "I knew it. I fucking knew it."

"I guess the question we need to ask ourselves is why? Why was that kiss so hot?" She knew the answer already. It was because they had chemistry, a connection.

It had been there from the beginning, before she had even understood it, or been willing to accept it.

But her question hung out there between them, impulsively asked.

He stared at her for a heartbeat.

"Am I supposed to know the answer?" Rick asked, reaching to her like he wanted to pull her to him, before he realized they were in public.

"Maybe someday," she said, a little disappointed. She wasn't sure what she had expected him to say. But yeah, she was disappointed. She wanted more than he had ever offered her or even hinted at. Hell, she'd already gotten more than they'd originally planned on. They'd been having stealth sex whenever they could, including another quickie the night before when River was with Rachel for a girls' back to school shopping trip.

She stepped away from the grill and went to spread out their tablecloth and clamp the edges so the wind didn't blow it away.

Rick lit the briquettes on fire and put the rack on top of it.

He came over and helped her pull out potato chips and a

salad she had made earlier and put in a plastic container. "Sloane."

"Yeah?"

He looked into her eyes. "I know what I *want* the answer to be. But I'm afraid if I say it I'll fuck everything up. You just got divorced and I have River and there's Sullivan to think about..."

Her stomach dropped. She bit her lip and opened her eyes wide because she suddenly felt like she might cry. He was giving her a "let's keep it casual" speech and she didn't want to hear it. "Got it." She turned and blindly walked toward River and Kate, needing to pet her dog so she didn't say anything else and make it worse.

As is, they could just keep the status quo. That was clearly what he wanted and while Sloane knew with all her heart she wanted more, she realized she needed to accept it for now. If she pushed he would pull away entirely and she knew from his sister he had plenty of women in the wings waiting to take her place in his bed. Or on his motorcycle.

"What's up, girls?" she asked River.

Rick had mentioned he and River were locked in a battle over her shampooing her hair and it was clear he was losing. Her hair was matted down and looked greasy and frizzy simultaneously. Sloane remembered all too well what it was like to be a girl growing up without a mom. Her own father had tried, but he knew nothing about fashion and ponytails. Sullivan had kept the house full of testosterone-laden boys and Liam had been more comfortable with that than with her tears over wanting to wear makeup at twelve years old. Maybe River needed a female friend.

"Nothing," River said, sitting down on the ground. "Come here, Kate."

The dog obediently went to her, tail wagging, and was rewarded with a head rub.

"Do you wish you had a dog?" she asked River, dropping down beside her on the grass.

"Yeah. Rick says no because we live in an apartment. I wish we lived in a house, but not like my dad's house. Like your dad's house."

That made Sloane's heart hurt for River. "That was a good house to grow up, that is very true. I think Rick is too busy to have a house though. He has the auto body shop and you to worry about, not fixing leaky toilets or cutting the grass."

"I know." River looked over at her. "Do you ever wish your mom didn't leave?"

Sloane wasn't sure how River knew that, but it was a small town and it wasn't a secret. "Sure, sometimes. But I don't really remember her, so I don't miss her. I just wished when I was your age and a teenager that I had a woman to talk to. My dad was great but there's just girl stuff sometimes."

River nodded. "I feel the same way. Rick tries, but he doesn't understand I'm growing up. And Rachel tries too, but honestly, she's more immature than I am."

Sloane smiled at River, amused by her response. "Well, I'm around if you ever need someone to talk to. I won't tell your brother what we talk about, I promise."

"Thanks. And you can talk to me, too, you know. About Rick. And how you feel." River's look was expectant.

Sloane was speechless. She seriously had no idea what to say. But then his words came right back to her. He didn't want to ruin anything. He didn't want anything more. She had to respect that. Keep things simple. Straightforward. Sex.

"I like Rick. We're friends, that's all." Why did it suck so hard to say that?

Because part of her had thought that if she wanted more, so would he. After all, he was the one who'd always had a crush on her. But that had nothing to do with his life as an adult and he liked the ladies. She was a friend with benefits. Nothing more, nothing less.

One benefit of being an O'Toole? She knew how to keep her emotions under wrap.

When Rick came over with Winnie and Todd, she had herself completely pulled back together. It was her first time meeting Todd and she stood up to introduce herself. "Hi, I'm Sloane, Winnie's new shampoo girl."

Not Rick's friend. Or Sullivan's sister. Or Tom's ex-wife.

She was Sloane, with a life of her own.

RICK WATCHED River run ahead of him at the Fish Festival, wishing like he always did, that she had more friends. It was worrisome. It didn't seem to bother her a whole lot but it just seemed to him that at some point she had to be lonely. Girls her age had sleepovers and put makeup on each other and watched the Disney Channel together. At least she'd agreed to go to camp for the next year, and now she had Kate to play with. A dog couldn't speak, but she could still be a friend.

He sipped a beer and lazily walked beside Axl, who was actually on-duty as a cop.

"I can see you worrying," Axl said. "She's a good kid, Ryder. You're doing a fantastic job."

He shrugged. "I do all right. But I do worry. I can't help it. And then I just get pissed at my dad. He bought her an iPhone without talking to me and now I have her watching YouTube videos in bed at midnight when she should be sleeping. And then to just totally embarrass me, he hit on Sloane."

Axl snorted. "You have to give him credit. The guy has balls."

"No, he has a dick and that's all he thinks with."

"Oh, and you're different how?" Axl gave him a side look. "You're kind of a player."

That ticked him off. "Hey, that's not fair." It wasn't. "I don't drag women into my shithole house and knock them up. I'm not like him at all." He resented the comparison.

"I didn't mean that. I meant you're so busy keeping women at a distance you're going to end up like him—alone."

"What are you, my fucking counselor?" Now Rick was flat-out angry because it hit a nerve. Sloane had hinted at something being between them at the park the other night and he'd pulled away. He'd given her the line he always gave women, about not wanting to ruin what they had by taking it further.

Her admission that she'd liked the kiss back in high school had been hot as hell, and deeply satisfying, but then he hadn't truly understood what she was asking of him. Then he'd tried to talk to her about it and she'd shut him down.

"River will grow up, go to college, and then what?" Axl held his hands up.

He had his damn cop sunglasses on with his uniform and Rick couldn't see his eyes. "I don't know." He hadn't given a lot of thought to it. He was just doing his thing. Living day to day.

Until Sloane had rolled back into town.

Now he had thoughts tumbling around his head he didn't know what to do with, and he'd tried to keep it casual and she had gone along with that.

He realized Sloane was standing next to River at a funnel cake stand. She had Finn on her hip. The festival was in downtown Beaver Band, and the lake was a beautiful backdrop for the sea of white tents and the carnival rides. Sloane was laughing, tossing her hair back, and adjusting Finn. He hadn't seen her since the park, but he had been texting her. Some flirty, some sexy, some normal friendship-type conversation. She had responded, sounded normal. But she hadn't initiated any in-person meetings.

It had only been three days and he missed her. How insane was that?

He didn't know what he wanted.

But he did know he wanted Sloane.

And he was scared to fuck it up. He didn't want to be his father. He didn't want to be that guy who runs through women, or worse, the guy who gets left behind.

"What am I supposed to do?" he asked Axl. "I think I might want something."

Axl peeled his sunglasses off and gave him a grin. "Something? Or Sloane?"

"What do you know about Sloane?" Rick asked, wanting to hear Axl's opinion.

"I know that you look at her like my father looks at my mother's lasagna."

Rick laughed. "Is that a euphemism?"

"Fuck no. I'm talking about my parents. I meant dinner."

That was how he felt about Sloane. He wanted to eat her. But was that just lust or more?

River ran over to him. "I'm going on the Ferris wheel with Sloane after I get a funnel cake."

He eyed his sister. "Here's a thought. Ferris wheel first, then funnel cake. I don't need you puking up fried dough."

That thought ripped him straight back down to reality. Sloane said she wanted a family, but did she want this kind of family? A guy who came with a kid as a package deal?

"Good call," River said, holding her hand out. She was rocking on her feet and looking super excited. "I need money."

He gave her a twenty and turned to Axl. "I'm an ATM.

This is why I can't get married. I'll go under financially if I add a wife to the mix."

It was a joke. But he was testing the waters, he knew it. He wanted Axl to give him permission to not be a bachelor. Which was stupid. He was a grown-ass man.

Sloane came over to him. "River wants to ride the Ferris wheel. Let me just wait for Lilly. She's in the restroom but she can take Finn."

"Where's Sullivan?" Axl asked.

"Beer tent." Her face showed her opinion on him drinking at noon.

"I see her coming," Rick said. "Here, give me Finn."

She handed him the baby and gave him a small smile. Maybe it was just his perception, but she seemed more remote now. Closed off a little.

Keeping it casual.

Fuck. He hated that.

He gave Finn a little bounce and told him, "Man, I hope you have your act together way before you're our age. We're a mess."

"Speak for yourself," Axl said. "I'm living the dream over here. I've totally got my crap together."

That was doubtful but Rick wasn't about to argue with him because he was watching Sloane get on the Ferris wheel with River. She spotted him and waved, a smile spreading across her face as she got settled in the seat.

A memory came rushing back to Rick.

It was the summer after Sloane's senior year. Eight months after the kiss. He had grown almost three inches and had started working out. Flirting with girls. Enjoying his rising social status.

Then he'd come to the Fish Festival with the guys and he'd seen Sloane on the Ferris wheel with her boyfriend and everything he'd gained in the last eight months seemed like nothing compared to what he'd lost.

He knew he would never have Sloane and that had crushed him like nothing else.

The Ferris wheel started moving and her long dark hair blew back.

God, she was beautiful.

He knew the answer to the question then, with total clarity.

It was love.

It hit him in the chest like a wrecking ball. Boom.

He was a complete and total idiot.

She'd been trying to tell him they could have a future together. That they both wanted the same damn thing. A normal family life with a partner you loved, and she'd been hinting that maybe, they should explore that option together.

He ran his hand through his beard, agitated. Holy crap, he had seriously blown it.

"Are you okay?" Axl asked him.

"No. No, I'm not. I'm a complete idiot."

"I could have told you that," Axl said, giving him a hard time.

"I need you to take Finn."

"Where the hell is Lilly? Or better yet, Finn's father?" Axl asked. "I'm on-duty. I shouldn't be babysitting."

Rick was watching the wheel turn around and around, knowing he had to be there when she got off of it. "Give me a break, seriously. Just take him."

Without waiting for an answer, he strode over to the Ferris wheel right as River and Sloane were disembarking.

"Hey, Sloane, want to ride with me?"

She shot him an amused look. "Um, I just got off the Ferris wheel. Oh, and hello to you too."

What had happened to all his years of easy flirtation and cheesy pick-up lines? He seemed to have forgotten all of it under the weight of the realization that he always had, and always would, love Sloane. "I have a ticket," he said.

She eyed him like he was losing it. "Okay, I'll ride it with you and River."

"River is staying with Axl."

"What?" River protested. "Why can't I go another time?"

"Because it's my turn." He had to do this before he changed his mind. The carnival sounds retreated and all he could focus on was Sloane.

"Ooooh," River said. "I get it." She made a heart with her fingers in front of her stomach where Sloane couldn't see it.

That made him laugh. He gave her another twenty bucks out of his wallet. "Go buy your funnel cake."

"You already gave me twenty dollars."

"You're not supposed to care."

River ran off.

Sloane's eyes had widened, her plump kissable lips parting slowly. "What is going on here?"

"I just want to ride the Ferris wheel. Do you know where Lilly is?"

"She's still in the restroom. There must be a line. But she can take Finn as soon as she comes back."

"I see her coming," Axl said. "Here, give me Finn and get on the damn ride before Rick pops a vein."

Axl knew what was up. Rick could see it on his face. His friend was grinning for all he was worth. Rick wasn't going to argue with him.

"Perfect." Rick took Finn and handed the baby off to Axl. Then he took Sloane's hand and basically dragged her back to the entrance to the Ferris wheel.

"Are you okay?" she asked. "And do you think we should be holding hands? Anyone might see us."

Rick stopped walking and turned back to her. Sloane collided with him.

"Oomph. Sorry. Why did you stop walking?"

"Someone might see this too and I don't care." Rick cupped her cheeks, bent down and gave her a kiss he felt in the depths of his damn soul.

She shivered when he pulled back. Her eyelashes fluttered and she glanced around nervously. "I'm really confused."

He wasn't. "I know why."

"What?" She looked at him blankly.

"I know why that kiss was so good in high school."

Sloane sucked in a small breath. "Oh, really? Why is that?" She pushed her hair out of her face and eyed him.

"Just ride the Ferris wheel with me and I'll tell you."

"Sure." She glanced back. "Lilly has Finn and River. That's good."

"That is good." He trusted Axl completely but he was on-duty. River was old enough to just stand beside the Ferris wheel and wait for him, but they were responsible for Finn since Sullivan was off being an idiot.

A few seconds later Rick was ushering Sloane onto the ride.

They were belted in and almost immediately they rose, not to load another swing but to rise all the way up into the warm summer air. They could see all of downtown and sailboats and fishing boats dotting all over the lake.

But truthfully, all he could see was Sloane.

"So what's your answer?" she asked, as she pushed her hair back off her face. She wasn't smiling.

He took her hand and laced his fingers through hers. Here went nothing.

"When I was fifteen the guys and I came to the Fish Festival at night and we ran into you here with your boyfriend."

She stared at him, looking a little puzzled. "I don't really remember that. But I came to the festival every year. What does that have to do with anything?"

"You don't remember it because it was no big deal. It was like any other day. But I stood down there and I watched you riding the Ferris wheel with what's-his-name and you were making out with him. And I told myself that I was a fucking idiot because I'd had that one shot. That one kiss in the dark bathroom and it was amazing. It was... everything. And I just let you go. I let you walk away and go on with your life and that night, I watched you with that guy, knowing you were leaving for college. And I swore to myself if I was ever lucky enough to have a chance with you, I would never let you go."

Sloane made a sound in the back of her throat. Her expression softened, her eyes growing glassy. "What does that mean?"

"It means that I don't want to be a secret. It means I'm an idiot for not picking up on what you were asking in the park. But I was afraid, you know? Afraid you like Rick the stripper and not Little Dickie. Afraid that somehow I'll become my dad, and I won't be worthy of you."

She turned as much as the car would allow her to and reached out and touched his face, running her hands through his beard. "I like *you*. The man inside. I liked you then and I like you even more now. I appreciate the muscles, but they don't make the man. Remember that. I watch you with River and it's amazing."

"And I see you with Finn and Kate and your family and those dogs at the kennel and I think you're amazing."

She smiled. "You still haven't answered the question. Why was that kiss so hot?"

"Because we're perfect for each other. Always have been."

Her eyes widened and suddenly there were tears there. He ran his fingers through her hair, drew his thumb under her eyes to ease the tears away. "I don't want to be just a guy who gets you off. I mean, I want to do that too." Fuck. He was botching this. "I want more. I want you. And me."

Her hair hit him in the forehead as they came around and were on the downswing. He held her hair down on either side of her face and he threw it all out there, just like the night he'd climbed in the bathroom window. She was worth the risk.

"Sloane, I love you."

FOURTEEN

SLOANE STARED AT RICK, disbelieving what she was hearing. Rick loved her? Like real love? Like what she was feeling?

This was unexpected and insane and totally irrational.

Or maybe it made complete and total sense.

Her body had known at seventeen what she had been too stupid and stubborn to see.

She and Rick were meant for each other.

He was staring at her intently, those green eyes dark and filled with love. He was squeezing her cheeks, hard, and she was getting dizzy from the Ferris wheel whipping back up into the summer sky, her legs dangling.

"Are you going to say anything?" he murmured.

There were a million things Sloane wanted to say. She wanted to gush and laugh and cry and ask him how they could do this. But then she realized all she really needed was to tell him how she felt. She nodded, raising her hands to place them over his. "Yes. I love you, too."

"What do you mean?"

"What do you mean, what do I mean?" She laughed. "I love

you. What response were you expecting when you said you love me?"

"I thought you were going to say you want to try dating out in the open." He studied her, eyes boring into hers. He kissed her. "I didn't think you were going to stay that. But damn, I am grateful."

Sloane closed her eyes and gave in to the wild freedom of the bucket spinning around and around and Rick's lips on hers, and love.

Unrestrained, unapologetic, love for a man.

When they broke apart, breathless, Sloane laughed. "The ride stopped."

They were one seat away from the exit platform and a glance down showed that a crowd had gathered. Her brother, Lilly, River, Axl, and her father were all there, watching them. Axl put his fingers to his lips and gave a loud whistle. Her brother shoved him. Her father was shielding his eyes against the sun and giving a little nod of approval. River looked smug. Lilly appeared astonished, holding Finn tightly.

"It did stop. And we have an audience." He dropped his hands. "They can say whatever they want and it still won't ruin this."

Except it wasn't words they used as they got down and walked through the turnstile. Her brother swung before either of them could react. She screamed, Rick managed to duck, but Sullivan still got him on the side of the jaw.

"What are you doing?" she shrieked, rushing her brother with a shoulder. They collided and went careening backwards into a garbage can. "Are you *nuts*? You have a baby two feet away!"

Finn had started to cry. River had big wet tears in her eyes and she looked terrified, clutching her funnel cake.

Rick was rubbing his jaw but he didn't swing back. He just said, "Sullivan. Back off, man. This isn't the time or the place."

"But it was the place for you to make out with my sister?"

Sloane grabbed her brother by the arm. "Get over here. Now. I want to talk to you."

"Get off me." He tried to shake her off but she held on tight.

She yanked him toward the back of the lemonade stand. "Thanks for making us look like a Jerry Springer episode," she snapped. "What is going on with you? Why do you care if I date Rick?"

Sullivan bent over and ran his hands down the front of his jeans. He took a deep, shuddering breath. "You don't understand."

"That's why I'm asking. We have to talk about stuff. For the first time in our entire lives, we need to talk about our feelings." She bent over too so she was more on his level.

He glanced over at her. "I miss Kendra."

Her heart squeezed. "I know. I'm sorry."

"I don't ever want you to feel this pain. I feel like I'm drowning. Like I keep grabbing for the surface and I can't find it. The current just drags me back under."

Sloane ran her hand over her brother's back, tears rising in her eyes. "But Sul, would you have rather never met Kendra? Would you have missed out on that love if you could have?"

He stood back up, pressing his fingers to his forehead. "No. I wouldn't."

"Then let me have that. I've never had that." Her voice caught. "I was married almost as long as you and I never had one one thousandth of that kind of love. I can have that with Rick. And if I get hurt, at least I tried. At least I feel *something*. I've been numb for years."

It was true. She felt like for the first time ever she was actually alive and living.

"Did it have to be Rick?" He pulled a face.

"Better him than some guy you won't like. Think how convenient this will be." She nudged him. "I won't interfere with poker night, I promise."

"Fuck. Are you really happy?"

She nodded.

"Damn it. Then I'm happy for you. The idiot has been in love with you since the tenth grade."

"Remember when he kissed me in the bathroom?" she asked, wanting her brother to understand. "I flipped out because the truth was it was the best kiss I'd ever had. Fireworks, baby."

Sullivan snorted. "Now that's funny. I have to admit."

"It is. Now let's enjoy the damn Fish Festival, please."

"I guess I have to apologize, don't I?"

"That would be helpful."

Rick was holding River against his chest and wiping the tears from her eyes. "Don't worry. Sullivan and I are still friends." He looked over at him. "Right?"

Her brother swallowed. "Of course. I'm sorry. That was out of line. If you want to date out of your league, go for it."

Rick laughed. "Thanks. I will."

Her father was holding Finn now and he looked at her closely. "You good? Everyone good?"

That almost made her roll her eyes. That emotion thing was going to take some working on in her family. "Yes, Dad. I'm good. And yes, Rick and I are together. So everyone just be happy and let's move on. Now I am going to go get a pickle on a stick."

Rick grinned. "You're so romantic, beautiful."

For some reason, she blushed. She made eye contact with him and she legitimately blushed. There was just something about the way he looked at her that made her giddy and she could not wait to be alone with him again.

. . .

RICK HELD Sloane in his arms and sighed in contentment. They were out on Axl's boat, enjoying a view of the Fish Festival fireworks being shot off a barge way out on the lake. The boat was gently rocking, the water inky, moonlight and the flares from the fireworks illuminating the surface. He was sitting on the back bench, Sloane between his legs, leaning against his chest.

Finn was asleep on Liam's shoulder, his little life preserver engulfing him.

River was reading a book by flashlight. Normally he would have forced her to put it away and enjoy the moment, but he was too happy to worry about it right now.

"On a scale of one to ten how happy are you right now?" Rick asked Sloane.

"An eleven."

That was the perfect answer. "Good. I'm an eight."

"What? Why only an eight?"

"Because we're not alone. We're going to have to figure out how to sneak away later," he murmured in her ear. "And have 'I love you' sex."

Sloane wiggled her body against his and turned to give him a sassy look. "I already had a pickle today. I'm good."

She'd come out to play. He laughed. "Oh, you're going to pay for that when I get you home."

"I can't wait."

Damn. She was everything he wanted in a woman, and then some.

Lilly leaned over several feet away and said, "I think we should make the charity event an annual thing. Sloane, you don't care if Rick does another Tap That Dancers routine, do you?"

"Of course not. It's for a good cause and he really, really likes to strut it."

Oh, yeah, she was practically begging for a spanking. "If you've got it, flaunt it," he said with a grin. "I'll just make it very clear I am off the market." He kissed the top of Sloane's head.

Forever.

"I've always been taken," he murmured in her ear.

"I love you," Sloane said with a fervor that made him want to take her below deck.

"I love you, too."

Sometimes, all you need to do is strip it down to see what was always there.

Thanks for reading STRIPPED DOWN! I hope you enjoyed Sloane and Rick's story.

Want more of the sexy TAP THAT guys?

STRIP SEARCH is out NOW with Axl!

An introverted rich girl.

A stripper cop.

And a live-streaming kiss that threatens both their careers.
Cop Axl Moore is pretending to be a stripper for charity. But the cute blonde pulled up on stage seems to think he is the real deal.

When Leighton, director for the reality show Wedding Crashers, gets stopped by a cop she swears is actually a stripper, she's determined to put the "f" in fun to save her job.

But their surprisingly potent kiss is caught on camera.

How do you recover from that?

With a fake engagement...

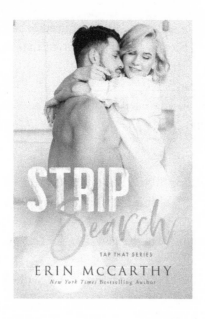

ACKNOWLEDGMENTS

Writing is a solitary job and I've been at this for over a decade now, which means I spend a LOT of time at home alone. I am so grateful for my tribe of author friends who keep me sane and help me sort out the voices in my head.

This series wouldn't exist if it wasn't for Erin Nicholas and Mari Carr and a dry erase board in Indianapolis. They encouraged me, brainstormed with me, and plotted this whole series out. And then threatened to kick my ass if I didn't follow through.

So here it is, book one, and I owe it to Mari and Erin. Love you, girls!

And to my readers who have stuck me through all these years, I am so completely grateful and humbled by your support. It means the world to me!

ALSO BY ERIN MCCARTHY

TAP THAT Series

Stripped Down

Strip Search

Strip Tease

ABOUT THE AUTHOR

USA Today and New York Times Bestselling author Erin McCarthy sold her first book in 2002 and has since written over seventy novels and novellas in romance and mysteries. Erin has a special weakness for tattoos, high-heeled boots, Frank Sinatra, and dive bars. She lives with her husband and their blended family of kids and rescue dogs.

Connect with Erin:
www.erinmccarthy.net